W9-BOO-676

BERLIN CANTATA

First published in 2012 by Haus Publishing Limited

HAUS PUBLISHING LTD.
70 Cadogan Place, London SW1X 9AH
www.hauspublishing.com

Print ISBN 978-1-907822-43-8
ebook ISBN 978-1-907822-42-1

Typeset in Garamond by MacGuru Ltd
info@macguru.org.uk

Printed in the United States

A CIP catalogue for this book is available from the British Library

to Gayle

BERLIN CANTATA

a novel by
JEFFREY LEWIS

To Lucy
Dear friend, so
good to see you.

JH 2012

"The Jewish migration to Germany, like other strands in the history of German-Jewish ties, is taking place amid a complex web of issues involving emotional questions of memory and forgetfulness, destruction and rebirth, politics and personal fate."

— *The New York Times,* March 23, 1992

DOROTHEA ANHOLT

Happiness

WHAT CAN I SAY? They sent me an invitation in the mail, I received it, I looked. What's this, I'm thinking. The City of Berlin, Germany? Now you get an envelope like that, with the cellophane and the whole thing, you immediately think it's a parking ticket, right? Of course it wasn't a parking ticket, it couldn't be a parking ticket, I hadn't even been a foot in that city in fifty years, and believe me, my memories weren't too great from then, as you can imagine. So I open it and I'm already aggravated. That's where it started. *They* invited *me.* Believe me, if they hadn't sent me that envelope, I wouldn't have gone.

I could bring a guest, I could go anytime to fit my schedule, the whole thing, I couldn't believe how nice they were, the plane ticket, the hotel. And I must say, you know I thought the hotel, if they were bringing over so many people, how could it be such a nice hotel? But the Intercontinental Hotel, no less.

How could you complain? Room service was good, the hotel was good. I bought a new piece of luggage. And then I had to decide. Should I invite Holly or shouldn't I? The invitation was you could bring two people, what was I going to do, go alone? I didn't even think she would want to. Always with the plans, my daughter, so many plans, here, there, she goes everywhere.

If you only have a month's vacation, an invitation from your old mother, I wouldn't want to impose, that's all.

But she was fine with it. "Oh Mom, of course I'll come, are you sure you want to do this, you can't go alone," on and on. So that was that. We picked the dates, and the people in Berlin, from the government, you almost couldn't believe how nice they were, they had one small change with the date, to fit the other guests who were coming, and that was that.

So we went. Boom. Just like that.

I didn't know what to expect. How could I know, I was just going, they invite me, so I go. And I have to tell you, that city has changed. Everything is just like new there. Now I'm not stupid, of course I knew it would be changed, of course, it was bombed, it had to be changed. But still you don't expect that. I was looking for all the things that I could remember. The zoo was still there. That was good, that was nice. And Wertheim department store? Those people were Jewish, too. A lot of people, a lot of things from then, were, of course. That was the whole problem. I don't want to even get into that. I didn't want to think about it. Just go, look, say thank you, go home.

Well that's what I thought anyway. But you see this is what daughters are for. Daughters are for aggravation. I'm barely unpacked, she's already nudging me, "When are we going to go to the country? When are we going to go to the country?"

"What country? Why country? We just got here. What, it's a whole city, isn't a whole city enough for you?"

The problem was, she had seen a picture, no, movies, we had a movie, which she found, I didn't even know it existed anymore, I mean you don't keep things forever, I thought it must have been thrown out, why wouldn't I have thrown it out? But she found it, of myself and my late husband, her father, in the country. We had a very lovely country house in the country, on a lake, and it was near there that we…

Well I will get to that. I'm getting to that. I don't quite feel like getting to that quite yet, but suffice to say, we had a very nice place on the lake and that was where we would go. My husband had quite a successful business, in mattresses and all kinds of bedding, everything to do with bedding, it was one of the larger shops in that area of commerce, and so we were fortunate. Martin loved the country. He would always talk about the fresh air, he had scarlet fever when he was a boy, I don't know if that had to do with it or not, but he always loved fresh air, we would go there on the weekend and he would stand outside breathing. You could see him taking big breaths. He looked almost like a giant, or one of these pictures at a nudist colony. It just made him happy to breathe the fresh air.

So anyway, that's what Holly was thinking about, that movie where we looked so happy. According to her, that is. But of course she didn't know the whole story.

I should correct one thing. I said Martin looked like a giant. But he wasn't really very tall at all. It was just the way he would stand outside breathing, he *looked* tall.

The part that Holly did know, this is what I was going to get to, I'm just going to say it, this is where, when the Germans came, I mean the Nazi Germans you know, but by then it just seemed like the Germans, because that's what they were saying, we're the Germans and you're not, anyway, I'm sorry, I'm losing my point – you know what I tell people sometimes, at my age, I'm going one way and my mind's going the other. My point is, simply, this is where we had to hide in the woods. We hid in this place, we never even knew what it was, it was either from the army from the war, or hunters, we never knew, we had heard different things, but it was cement and only above the ground by about two or three feet, a cement box, that's just what it was like, a big cement box, you couldn't even stand up, and that's where we hid. One year and four and one-half months, to be precise. Then they found us and that was that. Our darling daughter Helena perished on the train. Martin and I somehow were survivors but I'm definitely not getting into that.

Who's to say who's lucky and who's not? That's my feeling.

And believe me, I've seen more than I need to know.

But my daughter, I'm talking about my second daughter, Holly, she never lets a thing go, once it's in her teeth, she never lets it go, you could hit her with a stick and she would be holding on for dear life. She wanted to know all about the country. I said to her, "Holly, we're having such a good time. Here, here's the menu, order some room service." But no, her hamburger comes and still she keeps asking me. "Why did you keep it a secret from me? Who puts a film in a strongbox, anyway?" Oh and also, she wants to know why I'm having such a good time. I say, "Holly, it's not just me, did you see Mr. and Mrs. Bronstein?" They were with us in our van, they were nice people also, he was anyway, she seemed a little snob-bish, from Montevideo, Uruguay, no less. How did Jews get to Montevideo, Uruguay? I didn't even know that. But they were having a good time, too.

"The other people, the Shulmans, they're not having such a hot time."

"Well that's their problem." What could I say? It was their problem. I do understand. Of course, you could be bitter, but what's the point of being bitter with *these* people, they weren't even alive then, they're just trying hard to be nice, to say "I'm sorry." I accept that. I do. Who's to say who couldn't be in which situation in life? You never know.

Holly, shut up already. Of course I didn't say that. I don't talk like that to my daughter. And she did come all this way too, and giving up her vacation. She works too hard, really. I'll tell you this much about her: She's been living in Paris, France. Until recently she had a boyfriend who was quite nice, a dealer in art, things of that nature, but I don't think she really liked him very much. I wish she'd come back to California, not for my sake, absolutely not, for hers, I think it's good to live in your own country. Why? Because I don't know, but personally I think things are clearer, you always know where you are. She says she's going to, but is not sure when. She's a wonderful daughter, really. Never married. I can understand that. Of course, these days, nobody gets married, that's what it seems like anyway. I don't even bring up the subject of grandchildren. Why be heartbroken?

Anyway, it's her life. But what's good for the goose, that's what I was trying to tell her, this was *my* life, so if I didn't want to go to the country, why should I?

I think she thought it could be cathartic. I tell her, at my age, I don't need cathartic.

What I don't tell her, which I will only say once, right here, but only to be divulged after my death: I am ashamed of something. This is correct. There, I said it. And what am I ashamed of, Dorothea Anholt, eighty-one years old? If I could just tell you like that, it wouldn't be too big a shame, right? Of course not. Believe me, it doesn't work like that. If you're ashamed of something, you barely know what it is. Of course you *know* what it is, but you don't like to say it to yourself. You say it's something slightly different from what it is. This is my lifetime's experience, and believe me I don't need some expensive therapist doctor at one hundred dollars an hour to tell me this. For instance, I'll give you a perfect for instance: I am ashamed of what I am ashamed of. Because I don't think I'm ashamed of the right thing. I should be ashamed for my daughter who died. Or this is what I say to myself, Doe, you should be ashamed for that. But I'm not ashamed. Sad, yes. I am as sad as the day it happened. I'll never get over it. It happened, it's done with, but it's never done with. But ashamed? No. What's there to be ashamed of? We did whatever we could. We did our best. It wasn't good enough, God help us. So I think, it's something I could be ashamed of, probably I should be, but I don't know why. You could almost say, I'm ashamed for not being ashamed. It was the other people. They should be ashamed.

I shouldn't have even started this. This is what happens, you start something, with the best of intentions, and then what happens? I tell you, I'm going one way and my mind's going the other. There. I'll just say it, in one word: Ute. Ute is what I'm ashamed of. You can figure out the rest.

"But Mother, Herr Bruno says you can go to the country. The restrictions are lifted. We can get somebody to drive us out there. It's less than an hour." This is Holly again. She doesn't let up. She doesn't stop.

Finally I put my foot down. What can you do? You have to put your foot down. Who's the mother, after all?

I said to her, these words precisely, "Holly, if you mention the country one more time, I'm going home right now, straight back to Walnut Creek, no questions asked, the first flight."

"Fine," she said. Of course she would say that.

She went on to say that she didn't feel this city was too

attractive anyway, in fact she said it was as ugly as something, I don't remember what exactly, but as ugly as something that's ugly, that much I do remember, and so if I wanted to leave right now, this instant, fine, it was fine by her.

"Eat your hamburger," I said. It was a twelve dollar hamburger, even if we weren't paying, if she ordered it, she should eat it, right?

Anyway we didn't leave. But we also didn't go to the country. The next day we went to where Mama used to take me, on special occasions, I'd get dressed up and we'd go to Kranzler, the *old* Kranzler, for cream puffs. Every birthday, anything like that, or if we went to a museum or to buy new shoes, afterwards we'd go there. It wasn't the exact same, of course, this was the new Kranzler, they had a new modern building. I believe the old location was bombed. But we had cream puffs and they were so delicious. Mama used to say to me, it was like tasting a little bite of the moon. Everything came back to me, like in a flash. The day after that we left. Everyone was so nice, I just wanted to thank everybody. Herr Bruno was especially nice, a true gentleman. He was the one who showed us around and drove the van. He went where anyone wanted to go and he knew everything, even the old places that were gone.

OKSANA KOZLOVA

Wedding

HERBERT WAS A BIG CHEESE. His construction business was among the largest in the city. He was a trustee of the Jewish community. He was said to be among the city's richest men. He was sixty-four years old and had never married and so it was only expected that he would have a big cheese wedding.

He hoped to introduce me to Berlin society. He perhaps even hoped that I would find myself at home in it, or help him to find a home in it. This was unwise fantasy on his part. I don't condemn him for it, but it was unwise fantasy. I had only a passing, sociological interest in the kind of wedding he planned, in his villa on Schwanenwerder, with the Brazilian band and thousands of strung lights and all the men with their stomachs and wives with frosted hair. It would have been better if it had been in a movie. Then I could have walked in and out. But there I was, the star of the show.

I would say that while our marriage was not an altogether unlikely thing, yet, for all the logic in its support, it was strange. That is to say, there was an irreducible strangeness between Herbert and myself. We could come close, we could almost touch, you could even say that we understood each other, and then there would be a falling off, as back to our respective places we tumbled, with who knew what sort of divide or gulf or electrified fence between us. Surely part of it was due to our age difference. I have heard a Muslim rule of thumb that a wife should be half her husband's age plus seven years. In that case, I should have been thirty-nine or Herbert forty-six. If you do that little math puzzle, you will know the actual difference in age between us. And we came from different, if equally illegitimate, aristocracies. Herbert's one might call the aristocracy of suffering. He came out of the camps weighing forty kilos, an orphan of the war. This pedigree became a kind of virtue. If nothing else, it proved to the American occupiers he was not a Nazi. And he spoke English, and was not afraid of dirty work, and soon he was running a string of bars for the Americans. These bars, not surprisingly, specialized in prostitution. But Herbert was an honest whoremaster – on this I must take his word, yet I do. He has remained an honest man, from that day to this. It has been always a matter of honor with him, to show the Germans something, to refute the old lies. And, of course, that too brought him business. He bought up buildings that were still destroyed. He worked with his bare hands beside his workmen. He fashioned a life out of dust. Now enters into that life, many years later, the Soviet princess manquée. What else shall I term myself? My grandfather, my mother's father, was Comrade Brezhnev's munitions minister. It was he who raised me, after my father disappeared on a trade mission to Switzerland and my mother took flight to Finland. I led almost exactly the life that our criminal regime was instituted to abolish. I worked little, I flitted around embassy parties, I gained preferential entrance to university, I married a fellow child of the *nomenklatura* who believed only in Count Tolstoy, so we settled in a government *dacha* and lived a life of "purity" in the birch woods. Russian hippies, if you can believe such a thing. Our marriage, my first marriage, ended, but it was not because we were not bound at the hip. Quite likely it ended because we were. And then all of it ended, the regime, the privileges, the lies, and I wound up here, and with Herbert. I won't trouble you with certain of the details of how this came about. There was no "cute meet." But I will say this, about what divides us. Part of it has to do with "the Jewish question," or rather, the fact that Herbert perceives that there *is* a Jewish question, perceives it quite acutely, in Berlin in 1991. Whether he denies it or not, and sometimes he does and sometimes he doesn't quite, Herbert's life achievement is bound up with being a Jew in Germany, and with the peculiar wrestling with history that this begets. It's as though he's constantly saying, with his achievement, his power, his money: you haven't defeated us, not quite. Here I am, flying a certain kind of flag, the flag of Herbert, he seems to say. Whereas I, with my decades of Soviet education not all of which was lies, and perhaps even my inability to shed parts of it which probably were, don't particularly blame the Germans for anything, despite being what the Nazis would have called a "mischling." I continue to see the world as full of structural defects, historical defects, which produced the catastrophe of Germans killing Jews but many other catastrophes as well. The numbers matter to me, but I don't keep count that way. The Soviet Union was evidently not a competent instrument to correct these defects, but to deny the critique is to invite all such future catastrophes elsewhere. And so this business of "the Germans this," "the Germans that," as if fascism and the technical mastery of butchery were simply their home-grown crops for export, I don't buy it. I think it's sentimentality and hogwash and people whistling past their own moral graveyards. Well, much of it, anyway. There are some Germans I could do without.

In the meantime, one thing between Herbert and I is certain: we are both short. Standing together, I'm afraid we can sometimes look like a short father with his short daughter.

When I say the "wedding," what I am really referring to is our wedding party. Our exchange of vows was civil and private. I got through the vows by not listening too closely. It was the prospect of the big party which made me uneasy. I resolved to "stretch," to "make it work." These are ordinarily contemptible phrases to me, phrases a marriage counselor or advice column-ist might offer, so one could say it was a measure of my willing-ness to "stretch" and "make it work" that for this one night I embraced them. Herbert wanted a big bash, so I would stretch and see how this was important to him, to show me off, to make our debut. Herbert wished to invite his fellow business-men, so I would stretch and see how this was necessary and appropriate for business. Herbert spent money on this party that could have fed ten thousand poor, but I stretched and remembered that Herbert, too, had been poor, and the bitter-ness of it, and his glory in overcoming it.

And when you stretch towards another, you of course wonder if the other is stretching towards you. I could imagine Herbert being dismayed over some whom I invited. My students from the emigré center were of course the shabbiest, with their poor Russian clothes and clueless style. One could have hoped, because they were Russians, that they would drink too much and liven up the proceedings, but because they were also, all of them, either Jews or pretending to be Jews in order to obtain a German visa, they weren't really much good at loutish partying. For the most part they huddled together as if they'd just gotten off some immigrant ship, their eyes dazzled by the display around them. As for my other invitees, one was working up a story for his newspaper and the confluence of Berlin power brokers was convenient for him, another announced he would bring, as his "dates," his skinhead acolytes from the East, from Marzahn, in order to show them what the other half looked like, and then there was my new American friend, the only one I could point to who perhaps had no motive at all to be there except to wish me well. Or what am I saying? She doubtless wished to *meet* people. To none of these did Herbert raise so much as an eyebrow.

It was a warm September evening. The Wannsee sparkled in the moonlight. The thousands of little strung lights announced to all satellites, aliens, and deities above that right here on this spot on the earth something of note was going on. "Intelligent life," what a phrase, the pseudo-scientists' phrase. Our guests flowed out of the house, forming ever-shifting eddies and pools in the grass. Intrigues, romances, snubs, disappointments, all these doubtless were germinating, flowering, withering, everywhere I might have looked, but it was not mine that night to be too curious. I was floating above it all, saying my hellos, being kissed and danced with, paying as little attention to all of it as I had to my marriage vows. Herbert and I occasionally collided. I don't mean this in a metaphorical sense. He would go his way, I would go another, and occasionally we would bump. He wore a smoking jacket that night, and a foulard, and carried a cane. Later he would tell me how ridiculous he had felt, but I thought he looked the essence of himself that night, and quite dapper as well, and I was touched by it. Each time we were together, someone snapped our picture.

There then came the moment of the car. It was then that the vulgarity of the entire event came back to me with heavy force. Herbert had bought me a very expensive automobile, but as if that weren't enough, he had it driven out onto the patio so that he could present me with it. It was a silver Mercedes sports coupe with the largest engine imaginable, sitting there as if waiting to be filmed for a television advertisement. I am not one to blush, but there I was, skinny little Oksana from Moscow with the bad Russian teeth only recently fixed, blushing in embarrassment and rage. Herbert made a little speech, which truth be told he read in a monotone from notes, praising me and welcoming me. The five hundred guests who gathered around clapped politely as if bored. I felt called upon to say something. I had nothing prepared. I coaxed myself, I coached and urged, "Stretch, Oksana, make this work." But what came out was this: "Really, I have no idea how to drive this. In Moscow we took taxis. Herbert must want to kill me."

These were words that I heard first only when they were already aloft in the warm evening air. They hadn't preverberated in my mind. What dreadful words. People laughed nervously, then a bit more heartily. I laughed as easily as I could, as if to confess certainly it hadn't been the best of jokes, but it was, at least, a joke. This morale-building didn't quite work. At a little distance I saw Herbert, slunk into the background behind the car, laughing and clapping with the others. The eternal good sport, the avoider of the limelight, the puller of the strings. I ran inside as soon as it was feasible, and went upstairs where I felt no one else would go. The party went along smoothly without me. I watched from the corner of a window. It was a magnificent organism, a flowing dragon of humanity. The car still sat there, in the middle of it, rather ignored now, a kind of prop, beautiful yet jilted. Later I came down to say my polite good-nights to one and all.

Herbert didn't say a word about my cruel indiscretion. I knew that he wouldn't, nor would he hold it against me. Past midnight we wandered, more or less together, in the ruins the party left behind. Herbert is an optimistic person but not a happy one. Happiness must seem too dangerous to him. But he finds possibility in anything other than outright disaster. The party in his view had been a great success. The cleaners would come in the morning. "Was it not too unpleasant for you, Oksana?" he asked.

"Unpleasant? Of course not. It was fine."

"I'm glad you invited your friends. It would have been terribly gray without them."

You will observe the politeness and care in Herbert's speech. Sometimes I went along with this and sometimes not. I was still regretting my earlier cruelty. We mounted the stairs to the upstairs suite as if we were wandering ghosts. Jews had built the house in the twenties, Nazis had taken it in the thirties, leaving behind the hint of morbid Eros that pervades this entire city. It is like a fog, this hint, light and deft, coming and going, and it permits its inhabitants to behave like sleepwalkers or carnival goers in masks; love and death intertwined, invisibly. I contemplated an apology. Instead I took his hand.

Herbert accepted it with guarded passivity, holding it as one might hold the hand of a child while crossing a street. We were at the top of the stairs. The next stop surely was the bedroom, but it provoked in me no anxiety. I had little difficulty having sex with Herbert. I do not say this as a prostitute might. The absence of desire has its own beauty, austere, nearly colorless, like water. I don't believe I ever prostituted myself with Herbert, though I came out of Russia with nothing and in material terms he gave me much. He gave me my studio. He gave me the possibility of my own work. I had much to thank Herbert for, but gratitude was hard for me and sex has always been the coin of many realms. If he gave me little pleasure in bed, he was not alone. Long before Herbert, even going back to my first husband in the woods, I had developed an intricate fantasy that, coupled with the earnest thrashing on top of me, ultimately relieved me of my indifference. My old stand-by. A father goes away and then what? Go west, seek him out, even in the city that smells of death. But I can't divulge more. It would be unseemly to reveal what seems proper only in my own mind. Here you see my anti-Utopian tendencies. Now where would those have arisen? Of course a Prince Charming might come along one day and unlock all my secret lockets. But if I were Herbert, I would not be too afraid.

In the oversized bedroom, I felt that we were worse than merely short, I imagined that we might actually be "little people," people out of a Grimm's tale. Herbert not only built big, he redesigned big, or he had, until he met me. But there was nothing to be done about the high oak posts on which the bed sat, or the tall Venetian windows. I went to look out at the Wannsee. For easily the fourth or fifth time in the handful of nights we had spent here, Herbert, standing just behind me, pointed to a dark lump across the lake, quite identical to other dark lumps, and observed that it was the villa where the famous "conference" took place, that supposedly settled the Jews' fate. I nodded, nothing more, because I didn't care to find another fault with him by telling him it was the fourth or fifth time. It was then he told me how ridiculous he had felt in his smoking jacket and foulard.

For some reason I couldn't answer that, though I've told you how distinguished I'd thought he looked. "What a night," was all I said.

"Oksana…" I detected a pleading tone; never a good sign. He still stood behind me, touching my shoulders now. His light touch was slightly stronger on one shoulder than the other, as if urging me to turn around. But I was afraid.

"May I tell you a thought I never thought I would have? I think I would like to have a child."

Like a shot from behind, these words grazed my neck, causing it to burn.

"That's ridiculous," I said.

"What's ridiculous about it?" he asked.

"You never mentioned it once before. It must be this whole wedding fantasy that's gone to your head."

"I suppose…But I think of myself when I was young… I'm sorry, I never intended to trade so blatantly on my own suffering…"

"Let's go to bed," I said. I turned towards him. The pleading in his eyes overwhelmed me. He seemed, suddenly, defeated. I became furious. It was if he were interfering too far in my life, as if he felt he now had a right to. But I still would have said nothing more about it if he hadn't added:

"I know it wasn't part of our bargain…"

"What bargain? We had no 'bargain.' You think I would make a bargain with you? I wouldn't make a bargain with anybody. That's mad! You have this whole idea, now I see it, you've built it up in your head. You were waiting to spring it on me."

"Not at all," he protested.

"Lie! Liar! Of course you must have. Where could this have come from?"

Herbert looked dumbstruck. His eyes were wide with grief. I reflected on what I had said, and what he had said. "No.

I'm wrong. The bargain we had was that we wouldn't fall in love with each other. What a banal bargain. I can see that now. Would you say a bargain exists when no words for it exist but people behave over time as if they do? I think that's what you mean, isn't it?"

"I'm not so complicated as you, Oksana. My wants don't go away."

"Please answer me."

"You're cruel. Not to me, to yourself. That's what I can't bear."

"Thank you for the car," I said. "I'll learn to drive it."

We went to bed exhausted. Or really, I speak for myself. I had thought Herbert must be as well, but he pounded me in our sex that night as he never had before. He was relentless. He was in a rage. I thought he must be young. His relentlessness, first a distraction, became a facilitator of my fantasy. Finally I looked into his eyes, though I don't know what I saw there. It could have been love, but I wouldn't claim to know.

Afterwards, I showered and checked my birth control pills, to make sure that I had taken them.

HOLLY ANHOLT

Claim

MY MOTHER WAS CRAZY. That's one way to look at the evidence. Though it's funny that I should say that or think that, since I'm not really someone who believes in calling other people crazy. I save it for rare occasions, the way I save the little soaps that like a bag lady in upscale disguise I collect from hotels for times when I feel blue.

My mother was, perhaps, if not crazy, unrealistic? Though here too I would say: I'm not someone who necessarily thinks reality has sharp boundaries. It's there and then it's not there. Harsh critics somewhere will call me a relativist. Take my mother. Please. My mother who survived the extermination and never talked about it unless of course she had a sly conspiracy with my father to never talk about it *around me,* but secretly as soon as I left the room was talking about it all the time; my mother who was light-hearted and made jokes and lost a daughter on the "resettlement" train; my mother who was the most forgiving soul in the world; my mother who at age forty-two, the oldest mom of anybody I knew, had me to make up for it all. This mother who never spoke of the past for almost fifty years, then goes to Berlin at the city's invitation and goes around forgiving every German she can find and having the grandest time. There was no sign of Alzheimer's in my mother, either. She was sharp as a stick, could do the cross-word puzzles the whole week through. But what she wouldn't do, in Berlin, was go to the country. This was where she had hidden in the forest. This was where she had survived. It was also where their weekend house had been, and where they had been happy together. I had the pictures to prove it. Thirty seconds of black-and-white home movies, which I only found when they sold the house, because they'd been put away in a steel box, that showed my father in rolled-up shirtsleeves and my mother in a cotton print dress in a rowboat drawing up to a grassy lakefront. They must have been in their late twenties. He helps her out of the boat. Their feet get wet. They're carrying their shoes. They look towards the camera, she a bit bashful, he with a broader smile. A flower in my mother's hair. Shots, too, of a baby carriage and of their sprawling dark house. I wanted to go, I wanted to see, or I wanted her to see, as if I were her shrink honing in on a lively point of resistance. I wanted to break through what I thought was this crazy false-ness of hers, this princess childhood she was suddenly reliving. But she said no. Instead, when she died, in her sleep in Walnut Creek, California over the hills from San Francisco, she left me a claim that she had filed, in the days after our return from Berlin. It was for the country house and some property in Berlin proper. *Here*, if you're so interested, you deal with it, the claim seemed to say. She was buried beside my father in arid land made fertile by sprinkler systems and the bounty of the Sierras. For me her funeral was a tearless affair. The mourners were far from young, women mostly, friends from her bridge game or her volunteer work in Oakland, one black face as well, which at funerals like my mother's usually meant the maid, but my mother didn't have a maid. I stood a little apart, a late, hurried arrival, jet-lagged, on a bereavement fare. The only other relatives were an aunt from Toronto and a second cousin from La Jolla. At the time, I attributed my dry eyes, in equal shares, to exhaustion and the fact that I'd never been one to cry much. Even at the time I knew this was probably convenient rationalization. Such bits of wisdom as I've ever acquired pile up in my brain as if scrawled on so many little slips of paper, as if they were someone's recipes, and on one such slip was written indelibly what I'd seen on TV once, a lawyer telling how he won cases, and one rule was that you never let a witness give two reasons for anything. Two reasons are always a lie. The truth is always one reason. But I couldn't have said what that reason was. Most people, when their remaining parent dies, spend days or weeks sorting through what is left. I spent an hour stuffing a suitcase with mementoes and put everything else into storage. The obvious conclusion, that I couldn't deal with it, I dismissed with a slightly uneasy internal wave as pop psych presumption, like all the rest of the talk show shibboleths I hated to hear, get a life, lighten up, get past it, you just don't *get* it. Well, no, shut up, I begged to differ. A person can just want to get out of town. Later for the U-Stor-It in San Leandro. Later for the papers and the bank. Later for notes to various people who had shaken my hand. Later, too, for tears.

But for my mother's property claim in Berlin I somehow made a little time, as if for a guest from out-of-town that gets special attention for the distance she's traveled. A month or so after the funeral, I made my way back to this sprawling, shapeless metropolis, this sun-challenged L.A. of Mitteleuropa, to clean the matter up. I had little idea what to expect, other than I expected to leave soon. Then I met a fella. I stayed a little longer. In the meantime the claim plodded forward. I had two businesslike meetings with a lawyer, a woman with pronounced cheekbones, prunish mouth and a silver bun who had once been a formidable democracy advocate in the GDR. Anja Mann. Claims were Anja's money earner, or rather became her money earner after the collapse of the East German regime when it became possible for people who'd been dispossessed under the Nazis or Communists to file claims to get their property back. Soon claims were pouring in from the corners of the earth. My mother's, apparently, was among the first. She'd seen an ad in *The New York Times*.

My feelings at the outset about the whole business were anything but deep. I write this with the sort of confidence that sounds like another lie the minute I read it. I remember now being nervous every step of the way, nervous as the plane landed at Tegel airport, nervous getting my cheesy hotel on the Ku'damm and taking the lift up, nervous meeting the lawyer. Growing up in suburban California with everything normal and American except for two slightly elderly parents silent about their dreadful past, or what from a certain age of awareness I felt had to be their dreadful past, left me with questions, of course. The trip to Berlin with my mother had answered none of them, nor was it really supposed to. It was my mother's trip, not mine. But why was I even alive? I've written something silly on that subject already: "to make up for it all." I didn't actually know that. I knew nothing. And now there was this claim, this lawyer, my mother's death, and property that might be mine and might carry secrets: my reaction – my conscious reaction, as I suppose I should qualify it – was mostly to feel annoyed at the imposition on my time and attention, and to wish the whole thing would go away. It might have, if I hadn't met Nils. I would have signed a few papers, looked around a bit, and flown back to Paris. Months or years later, a check would have shown up in the mail or it wouldn't have.

But I did meet Nils, which I'll either write about later or I won't. I met him through my lawyer, actually.

It was on account of Anja that I met the Russian painter Oksana, and it was at Oksana's wedding that I met Nils.

Some other fairly irrelevant factors: I marveled at my lawyer's ability to evoke ambivalent feelings in me. If she ever smiled, they were forced, unlovely smiles, as if she were suppressing the taste of something she had eaten. She lacked cuddliness altogether. She gave the uneasy-making impression that if you weren't with her, you were against her. Yet anything I could think to ask Anja Mann, she could explain. And patiently – she seemed to like to explain, she seemed a little schoolmarmy. I felt in good hands with her. She asked me at our first meeting whether I wanted an actual return of my parents' properties or simply a cash settlement. I said cash. And then it was she, on the day after Oksana's party, who called me at my hotel to tell me about the rival claim. "I've been trying to reach you, Miss Anholt. We must go to a meeting. Are you free Tuesday afternoon?"

"Of course. What's going on?"

"Someone else is claiming your properties. A family whose name is Schiessl."

Of course I'd never heard of them.

She continued: "The people claiming...I'm not sure how to present this to you, it's rather strange, really...I haven't had a case similar...They're the family to whom your father was forced to sell, when these properties were 'aryanized'."

"Nazis?"

"I believe so. Former Nazis."

The words caught me by the throat. "I don't know that I want to walk into a room with former Nazis. Former Nazis, still secretly Nazis…"

"Well of course. I can represent you. That shouldn't be trouble. I'll go. I'll collect information. Then we'll talk."

"No."

"No?"

"No," I said again. "I'll come. I'll be there."

Hard for me to explain this quick reversal except as evidence of counterphobia, yet it had never been true before that I ran in the direction of my fear. I decided I was doing it for my mother. I imagined that she was brave, and that it was necessary that I be like her.

Another lawyer's office. Anja's had been bright, airy, designed, a show of contemporary relevance. This one was musty and indifferent, as if the law moved more slowly here, through a more humid atmosphere, a place where you'd expect a ceiling fan to be groaning. In the elevator she had said, "You need not say anything. Speak only with me," a cue that could lead one beset with uneasiness but not wishing to be seen as weak to do pretty much exactly the opposite.

The other lawyer wore a sport jacket rather than a suit. He was thin with thinning white hair and close-set eyes and there was something androgynous in his manner. It's possible his handshake was too pleasant. I didn't like the fact that he wore a sport jacket instead of a suit. Was he not taking my case seriously? His name was Rosenthaler. Like Anja, his English was efficient, university-trained, although he had the habit of prefacing or concluding any utterance where it halfway fit with *ja*, as if this were the one word in German which I was sure to understand.

"Are the others coming?" Anja asked.

"The Schiessls? No. The Schiessls won't be here." Rosenthaler's thin fingers picked briskly through his file. "My principals are eighty-seven and eighty-three respectively. Just let me get these things together. Let me explain the situation…"

He pulled out whatever documents he was looking for, three or four sheets of onion skin paper, then addressed me directly. "Our understanding, Miss Anholt, is you have filed your claim for these properties. The Schiessls have also filed their claim."

It was a moment when I loved my lawyer's wince, as if it were exactly mine, as if for a moment we shared the same face. "With all due respect, the comparison is absurd. Between a Jew holding proper pre-war title and people who benefitted from a forced Nazi sale?"

"*Ja, ja,* of course," Rosenthaler conceded. "But kindly examine this." I recall the hushed sibilance of the onion skin sheets as he passed them across the conference room table. Anja took them and studied them for what seemed too long a time, her eyes with metronomic efficiency clicking up and down the pages. All I could make out was that the edges of the paper were brown, like a cake that had been baked too long. Finally: "Would you recognize your father's signature, Miss Anholt? Is this it?"

She turned the aged papers so that I could examine them. My eyes ignored the German text and went directly to the unevenly blue-inked name at the end of many dense paragraphs. There was something modest to my father's signature, it seemed almost too legible, with its broad strokes and full loops, as though good penmanship and good citizenship were thought by its author to be related, valued things. But I also imagined: it was a signature not difficult to forge. "It looks like it," I said.

"Can you read the German?" she asked me.

"No."

"Then I'll explain. This document purports to be a sale, agreed to between your father and the Schiessls, in which your father gives to the Schiessl family for four thousand five hundred dollars U.S. whatever rights he may have had in any of these properties. And it's dated 1947, years after the Nazis fell."

I stumbled towards the obvious, feeling the beating of my blood. "So what does it mean?"

Attorney Rosenthaler was ready for that softball. "Please, let me explain why we're here. The Schiessls' claim has its own problem. They themselves were expropriated in 1948, *ja*, when East Germany was under direct Soviet occupation. But the new claims law provides compensation only for expropriations under the Nazis, until 1945, or after the East German government was instituted, from 1949."

"So they have no rights to compensation at all." Indignation came easily to Anja Mann, her cheeks flush, her voice low and sure. "Their claim's worth exactly nothing."

But Rosenthaler mocked her words slyly: "Not exactly nothing, I wouldn't say."

"They were expropriated by the wrong government in the wrong year. Yet they're willing to use this paper to prevent Miss Anholt from getting anything? That's quite astonishing."

"Not astonishing at all. Why astonishing? Schiessls and Anholts concluded an arms-length transaction in 1947, *ja*? Mr Anholt gave up his rights freely... But what if this paper didn't exist?"

By then I may have been having one of those out-of-body conversational experiences where you look down from the ceiling and say "What's *she* doing here? Are they talking about *me*?" But Rosenthaler was eager now, his ingenuity ready to have its day. "The Schiessls have a proposal. Let us, in effect, tear up this paper. You pursue your claim, Miss Anholt. And if and when it's successful, you and the Schiessls split the proceeds."

"I don't want anything to do with this." I pushed my chair back, stumbled up, the way you're supposed to when you've finally had it with something. "No! I won't become partners with Nazis."

In the elevator, Anja was a fount of mollifying words, comforting words, which despite the surprising warmth of her tone were a challenge for me to pay much attention to. I was too busy convincing myself I'd really been offended: "I don't believe it. I don't believe my father would do business with Nazis."

But even then I was thinking of the onion skin paper, that you never see anymore. My father always had a big box of it. It was the only sort of paper he ever used. It went with his Remington typewriter, the box would come out whenever he typed a letter or a bill of sale, as much a part of the mystique of him as the Oldsmobiles he bought every other year, like clockwork, and proudly washed in the driveway every Saturday afternoon because that's what Americans did and he was an American now, even as the sweet, decayed scent of his German-language books, the Goethe and Schiller that must once have been his household gods, still lingered in his study.

At a loss, I met my friends Oksana and Nils at the old Café Charlie on the Friedrichstrasse near Nils' office. I will say exactly three things about Nils: one, he was a reporter; two, he was one of those tall, lanky types with a long head, kind of a bearded Viking marauder turned aggressively, prematurely gray; three, he'd gone out with a number of Jewish girls before me. You might say we were his specialty.

Confused, overcome with the sense that a naïve, Disney-drenched upbringing was surrounding me like fairy dust and obscuring the world as it really was, I laid out the facts as I understood them to my new friends. "I could file my claim, I could get everything and then these people, these *Nazis*, could come in and get everything from me."

"What does Anja say?" Nils asked.

"Well she says they won't. They'll promise not to, because otherwise why would I even file a claim? They need to share with me. But I don't know. I don't know anything. Even if any of this is legitimate."

"Did your father keep business records?" Oksana asked.

"That's what Anja suggested – to look, you mean?"

"I don't know," Oksana said, "But if you want to be sure…"

If there were business records, they would have been in San Francisco. The left side of my brain made a disappointed calculus of my frequent flier miles while the rest of it wondered if I should at least be smoking a cigarette or ordering something other than tea, if I wanted them to think I was less a child. Nils sat crosswise in his chair, more facing Oksana than me, so in control of himself that I could barely stand it.

"You both think my father did it, don't you?"

"You make it sound like a crime," Oksana said.

"Do you really think a nice Jewish man, three years out of Auschwitz, with a daughter dead, a wife traumatized, would make a deal with Nazis for money?"

But my words sounded rhetorical, as if I were rehearsing something, and I knew the chance I could come out wrong on this. After all, what was truly astonishing to me was not that my father would accept, but that such an offer had been made in the first place. Nazis making postwar deals with Jews? I had never imagined such a thing. But Daddy was a practical man. My mother said this so many times about him, usually in apologetic tones, as though "practical" were an antonym to spontaneous or joyful or easy.

Nils kept his silence awhile, having the habit which I've found to be not universal, particularly among European men, of wanting to be sure of something before he ventured in, then finally he said: "Probably the best thing your father ever did. It was what he could do to overcome humiliation. It was noble. It was hard. Your father was a saint."

So, in the opinion of one individual who at the moment was way on my good side, my father was a saint. I tried to imagine my father humiliated, as though standing there with egg dripping down his face and onto his clothes. With nothing he could do about it; a fertile egg, a pinprick of blood. And then others, like Nils, recognizing my father's humiliation for what it was, not letting it go in secret, saying it, speaking it out loud.

One week later I was on a plane to San Francisco. I skipped the nostalgia tour of Walnut Creek and drove my rental directly to the U-Stor-It. There, in a chainlink locker the size of a jail cell, surrounded by boxes of my parents' possessions that howled accusations of neglect, I again opened their metal strongbox and found, underneath the camp photos and report cards, in a packet of documents held by string, a second original of the quitclaim document I had seen in Berlin. This time my father's watery, clear, childlike signature reminded me of him sitting in the back room of the office supply business he had built for twenty years behind a thick-legged oak desk that always seemed a size too big for him writing check after check out of a ledger checkbook. Never complaining. He didn't seem to have a huge amount of money, but just enough. Like the Henny Youngman joke, old Jewish man gets hit by a truck, he's lying in the gutter, ambulance on its way, the cop comes, balls up his jacket, puts it under the guy's head, asks, "Are you comfortable?" Jewish guy says, "I make a nice living, thank you." And then he died, and I myself had just enough, a couple thousand extra a month, anyway, so that now I could do crazy, unscheduled things like quit a good job in Paris or go to a city where I knew no one and had never had a desire to be or fly halfway across the world to prove the obvious.

I browsed further, as a delaying tactic as much as anything, or a distraction from what I felt as a defeat. And soon I found, among copies of life insurance policies that had lapsed, and expired warranties, and letters from the Naturalization Service dated 1953 congratulating my parents on their American citizenship, an escrow agent's receipt for the down payment on our house in Walnut Creek. It was for the same sum the Schiessls paid him, four thousand five hundred dollars. The escrow payment was dated the seventh of October, 1947. The agreement with the Schiessls was from three weeks before. He had used the Schiessls' payment to buy the house that I grew up in.

The storage bin felt like my home then; or the place out of which I had hatched, a hermit's place, where I could sit all day in wan fluorescent light wondering if Jews had saints. I called Anja Mann in Berlin to tell her to make the deal with the old Nazis, my new partners.

Then one night after returning to Berlin I drove with Nils to the GDR countryside to try to find my parents' country house.

I hadn't looked at my film in awhile, yet I felt I remembered enough of it that I would recognize the building. We got lost. The roads were terrible. Nils lost his temper in a childish way I found endearing then frightening then endearing again. At dawn or near dawn we found the hamlet of Velden am Moritzsee, though nothing said Velden and no sign announced the Moritzsee. There were inky patches of a lake through clearings in a dense wood, and unkempt stucco houses built back from the road or set down at odd angles to it, home to Trabants and chickens and multiple families. Each house I compared, in what felt like an act of desperate love, to the images that seemed teasing and fleeting in my mind. Not this, not that, like the mythical sculptor I chipped away at memories that were not even mine. I was so grateful when I saw it. It was as if it was still enough the same, as if it were allowing me to remember it. Rusted iron gates, like old retainers that could no longer be afforded and would be there until they died and then never be replaced, buckled at each extremity of a shallow scooped drive. The house itself stood back from the road perhaps twenty yards, among poplars and birch, hulking in the half-light, dark and colorless, its pitched roof like its neighborhood feminine and familiar, and at one end the telltale sunroom with its expanse of glass, raised, as the land sloped away, on an exposed concrete foundation embedded with stones the size of coconuts. A couple of bicycles lay in the grass. A cat scurried away.

Anja Mann had told me a little of what to expect: the GDR had converted it into a writers' retreat. The East German writers union had held it.

We peered in through one set of gates, our noses close to the posts.

"Climb over?" Nils asked.

"Just look."

"Probably best. No point scaring people."

"I guess they're still living here."

"Do you know how many?"

"No."

"The union's sycophants and Stasi informants, for sure… I'd have no regrets throwing those jokers out."

"Look!"

"What?"

"That birdhouse. It's in my film."

It was just then, I believe, that I imagined for the first time the possibility of possessing this house, of it being mine as it had been my parents'. Or even more oddly, of it being properly mine, of it being in some half-lit sense my inheritance. A girl finds a film in her parents' strongbox and passes it through the incandescent halo of her mother's bedside lamp, squinting to ward off the glare, seeing little. Numbers. Seven-six-five. Three-two-one. Then what might have been a lake and what might have been the sky, or the other way around. It began there and now I was here. For a few moments, I forgot about my partners the Nazis.

ANJA MANN

Joke

ALRIGHT, I'LL SHARE A SMALL JOKE. Or perhaps it's not a joke at all. Perhaps only someone such as myself could think it was a joke. When I gathered the paperwork together regarding the claim of the elder Mrs. Anholt, inherited by her daughter, I recognized at once the property described as the old East German Writers Union retreat in Velden am Moritzsee.

I knew who was living there and who might be evicted if the claim came to fruition. This provided, shall we say, a delightful added motivation, above and beyond my customary fees, to see the claim through to a successful conclusion. Of course, it would have been inappropriate to share this motivation with my client.

Screw yourself, Simona Jastrow. Be homeless, for all I care.

HOLLY ANHOLT

Atonement

I MENTIONED PREVIOUSLY that it was through Anja that I met Oksana and it was at Oksana's wedding that I met Nils.

But the circuits were busier than that.

The day of my second meeting with Anja, she invited me to her apartment for something which she described as "a little gathering." It turned out it was to mark the conclusion of Yom Kippur. I hadn't known it was the Jewish holy day. But here in the old East Berlin, on the fourth floor of a mouldering apartment building on a leafy, cobblestoned street, people were gathered to somehow take note.

It could have seemed like a little cabal, the thirty of us there to break a fast when few of us had been fasting, Jews coming out of nowhere, as if responding to a call that only they could hear, "Communism's finished. Come on back. Check it out." There was even a close-shaven rabbi from Illinois who fashioned himself a missionary. "These people wouldn't know the Day of Atonement from Income Tax Day." His mantra went something like that, and probably it was so. It certainly might have been so of me, if I'd known exactly what he meant by "Income Tax Day." But then it turned out the mantra was mostly prologue to an invitation to dinner, which I declined, citing jet lag, though I'd only flown from Paris. As for the rest,

I was bewildered. A city without Jews that had all these Jews in it, or this many anyway, enough to make a party of plastic cups and wine out of jugs in an apartment that if you squinted might have been on the West Side of Manhattan up by Columbia. Remnant Jews, secret GDR Jews, a few Soviet Jews. Jews who'd fled and come back with the victors, Jews who were lost mandarins now, Jews who'd believed in the universality of man and maybe still did.

It was as if one crisis of faith was begetting a flirtation with another, and as if the city that had lost one of its limbs was receiving a miraculous gift, a little bump under the flesh, where the limb was just beginning to grow back. Faith and miracles, not really things I knew much about.

But so many people who came to be what the city itself would be for me, its human geography, its insisting pulse, were there that night. Oksana, the beautiful Franz Rosen, and sweaty David Fürst. And Nils, who came late with David. Somehow we didn't meet then, but I saw him across the room, spare, reserved, cool, not talking with anyone, or seeming to want to. It may have been on account of that first night that always afterwards I would dream of him with one hand in the pocket of his jacket. His left hand, holding something, holding something back.

DAVID FÜRST

Enterprise

MY ROUGH REACTION to all the Jews arriving from Russia was, get out of here, this is my turf. Go home, go to Israel, go to New York, what's wrong with you? Of course I knew the many reasons why they came here. In Israel you'd have to serve in the army and there were many other inconveniences, including the possibility of being bombed on a bus. America had more restrictive immigration laws and less socialistic political arrangements. By comparison, Berlin felt oddly familiar. Germany was close by, prosperous, free, and best of all, it was welcoming. To go by our government, it actually wanted its Jews back. Well, it couldn't have *its* Jews back, of course, but it could have substitute Jews. So the unlikely tripartite emigration developed, to Israel, to America, to Berlin. My objection was entirely personal. I wrote about this in my newspaper. For years I had made a nice living, thank you, being the lonesome Jew in the land of the murderers, describing the hills and valleys, making my accommodations, being ironic like crazy, fitting in, doing well or well enough. These new immigrants were turning me into a commonplace. If things went on like this for ten more years, Berlin would be a normal city, Jewwise and otherwise. David Fürst begins to see his redundancy. I wrote a last column about it all and resigned.

This was more a dramatic flourish than a fact. I agreed at once to do occasional guest columns. In the meantime, I believed I had found a way to stay ahead of my brethren from Russia and to keep myself relevant. One of my columns a few months before had been about the skinhead effulgence in the East and the efforts of a Lutheran minister to do job-training among the right-wing youth of Marzahn. Shortly after my column ran, the minister ran off to Casablanca with a male schoolteacher he met on the job. This did little to enhance the confidence of his skinhead charges in the sincerity of the West. I saw an opportunity to step into the breach. If these little right-wing savages wanted job training, why not receive it from a Jew? I had been a car enthusiast and amateur mechanic most of my life. You may have already noted a certain working class coarseness of grain in my personality. I should say that this has been equal parts my *shtick* and my desire. To be not superior to my pipefitter father, to not try to show him up, against and admixed with all my reflexes to rise in life. To embrace the romance of manual labor, to be a muscle Jew, not a lump in a chair. As well, I suppose I was eager to show, to whom exactly I couldn't quite say, what a Jew could do in the love-thine-enemies area. So a mid-course correction in career seemed as seductive as it was practical.

A sensible Berliner of my generation, I did the first thing any of us did whenever we came up with a fresh idea: I looked around for a grant. An acquaintance of mine, a recent émigré herself, had recently become affianced to one of Berlin's richest men. She persuaded him that his foundation would do well to toss a bit of seed money my way. I rented a warehouse in Marzahn and began recruiting from the swirling local pool of bitter, racist, disillusioned, neo-Nazi little shits a crew of the least objectionable to be apprentices in my program, which would teach them not only about the various Western model cars they were unfamiliar with, but a handful of capitalist business skills as well.

In a word, the program went badly. I managed to sign up, from among the absconded pastor's former charges, four reasonably bright, appropriately shorn, politically questionable apprentice mechanics. I bought up various junkers and shop manuals for us to work from. We set up regular hours for study and practice. We opened our doors. We advertised. Our rates were dirt cheap. But no business walked in the door. Part of our problem, of course, was that we were in Marzahn, where if the citizenry had cars at all, they were mostly Trabis, which needed repairs often enough, but for which, on account of the chronic problems, there was no shortage of experienced hands to fix them. But I couldn't afford the rent anywhere in the western city, and it would have been a long, strange commute for my charges in any event. So we were slowly going bust, until what seemed a miraculous brainstorm arrived to save us.

It seemed miraculous to me, I should say, not only for its timely appearance but on account of its source. Richard Kunstlinger was a bony, watery-eyed boy of nineteen with a pencil-thin nose that reminded me inevitably of my favorite needle-nosed pliers. He had come into a wreck of a Trabant on his father's death. Before joining my project, his chief experience in car repair had come from attempting to restore to roadworthiness this modest, ruined example of the East German economic miracle. One day he drove his father's Trabant to the garage. It made the immediate impression of being a clean piece of work. It didn't belch or hiccup. Even the windshield wipers were attached. We all looked under the hood, medical interns with a new cadaver to consider. What struck me at once was not only its resplendent cleanliness – you could have cooked and eaten the mythical fried egg off its exhaust manifold – but the presence of a gleaming, unfamiliar part, like a chick from a different species in a nest, in the already tightly-packed engine compartment. "What's that? What's that doing there?" I asked.

"It's a catalytic converter," Richard said, nonchalantly.

Richard had deduced how to adapt the catalytic converter of a wrecked 1987 Opel in order to reduce the emissions of his belching, smoking, hyper-polluting old Trabant to the point of near invisibility.

I asked him how he did it. He was nonchalant about that as well. He said it had been mostly trial and error, he'd tried out several junkyard converters, determined to make a clean machine.

I praised him lavishly, then announced to the entire group: "I believe Richard here may have saved our skins, pardon the expression."

My charges grumpily granted me a minute to explain myself. "Why are we beating our heads into the wall? We're in Trabant country, we're surrounded by millions of the little beasts. Currently, of course, they're despised, ignominious, laughable symbols of your former wonderful government's disaster. But what if we, and we alone, came out with a clean, pollution-free Trabant? Wouldn't we be in the forefront of the inevitable GDR nostalgia, wouldn't we have a cult car?"

All four looked at me askance, or with incomprehension. The tools and lingo of the capitalist huckster were still blissfully foreign to them. I repeated myself and explained. Finally, with nods and grunts but mostly silences, they indulged me to the point where I believed they must be allowing me enough rope to hang myself. I went immediately back to the Herbert Kaminsky Foundation, begging for enough money to begin production on pollution-free Trabi cult cars, praising the talent and initiative of my young skinhead apprentice who had thought up the whole scheme, thereby showing fine capitalist instincts waiting to be exploited. I walked away with enough cash to buy a dozen worn Trabis and every mid-eighties Opel catalytic converter to be found in the city's junkyards.

Now all seemed strewn with roses for Skin Enterprises, but what of my relations with my charges? I confess that at the outset I had a hard time differentiating them, as if they had been sculpted ensemble out of a single block of wood. There was Richard, whom I've briefly described. In some ways he seemed the runt of the litter. He was the only one about whom you couldn't have confidence that he could easily beat someone up. There was an angularity about Richard, an inability to face you at anything but a slightly oblique angle. I had no idea, ever, what he thought. And he had skinny arms, unsuitable for street combat. Heinrich and Hermann were more obvious characters. If they hated you, they hated you, end of story. Blubbery and pin-eyed, they were the types you could make beer commercials from, men of definitive but dull opinions, masters of the quick but fatuous comeback, easily amused. I particularly liked Heinrich's raucous, gut-choking laugh, which could be aroused, for a typical example, by any joke whatsoever about a homosexual. Finally there was dear Johann. Johann styled himself the group's leader. He felt that he earned this mantle by being the quickest to criticize me for any failing. He was also the most physically imposing, tall, muscular and rangy. I might have done better to train him as a prize fighter, some new "white hope," quick but not quite quick enough, whose guts some black man might decorate a wall with. Johann's intellectual framework was to take anything the GDR had ever taught him and believe exactly the opposite. This simple schema also facilitated his desired ascendancy over his fellows: for every question, he had a ready answer.

I could have done with less of Johann. In fact I might have given him the boot, but for the saving grace that he was greedy. He was the only one of the four who seemed to have any interest in, or instinct for, making money. Since adaptation to the new economic environment was the aim, you could see that he provided a promising, if not strictly necessary, component to the whole. Our typical day ended with a session of self-criticism. What this meant, chiefly, was that I criticized them, or they criticized me, or they criticized each other. None of us, yours truly included, showed too great enthusiasm for criticizing themselves. I criticized their laziness, their sloppiness, their tardiness, their snarliness, their indifference to quality, and their not infrequent alcohol breath. I left their politics alone. They, particularly Johann, criticized my bossiness, my intrusiveness, my loud mouth, my sarcastic put-downs, my pudginess, and my failure to make them immediately rich and successful. They never referenced the fact of my Jewishness, though of course they knew it well enough, from my public newspaper columns if nothing else. Instead they indicted me as a journalist. According to this theory, I was someone who would inevitably betray them in print. Even if the project failed, I would write a book about it, or more columns, and have my own success. I didn't give a shit about them except as material. I would forget all about them.

This, of course, was rather shrewdly reasoned on their part. I could hardly deny the possibility.

I had hoped our orgy of self-criticism might dissipate with the success that Richard's innovation would bring us. But success proved elusive. We built six "clean" Trabants yet sold none of them. And our failure begat more doubts. I was accused, not by Johann alone, but by Hermann and Heinrich as well, of being naïve, stupid, grandiose, and clueless about the capitalist world I'd supposedly lived in all my life. My counterpoint was to suggest that the door was wide open, they could quit anytime they wished, or we could close the shop down and they could go to hell. But none of my critics quit. Either I was their main chance or they found me oddly interesting or they were gathering evidence against me. A father figure, that's what I really was, and a rather patient one when you came right down to it, who permitted them to vent their bottled fantasies of rage. I supposed I had them where I wanted them. Richard alone refrained from grumbling, a restraint which I attributed only to my own recent extravagant praise of his inventiveness.

How to move our fine product? I wrote more columns, I teased my friends, I applied social pressure wherever I could. Finally an American woman rose to the bait. She had a recent inheritance, she needed a car, she'd recently taken up with a friend of mine, she probably thought she was doing some good. I had been plying her mercilessly with my store of aphorisms which scared the shit out of her, "The Germans have never forgiven the Jews for Auschwitz," and so on, and she must have felt that if she became my customer I would let up on her. Little did she know that I'm said to be even more obnoxious with my friends. So we sold her a Porsche-red Trabant then voted unanimously to use the entire proceeds to buy alcohol and have a drop dead drunk party. Why invest wisely when you can celebrate your limited success today?

The party took place in the warehouse. After several hours of carousing, it came to recriminations and blows. Here at last the word "Jew" and the phrase "Jew pig" entered our polite conversation. No offense taken, I returned most compliments with equal or better. At one point I whacked Johann in the kidneys with a large wooden mallet. During most of the goings on, Richard Kunstlinger maintained a curious reserve, speaking little, drinking less. He became an observer more than a participant. No amount of jollying or teasing could engage him. Through a stale haze I became aware that this was pissing me off. What right had Richard to cop a superior attitude? One puny bit of innovation? I observed him at one point sitting cross-legged on the shop floor, hunched slightly forward, his watery eyes watching the rest of us through the frame of his upturned toes. He seemed fatigued.

The next day everyone showed up for work. This wasn't so large a feat as it might sound like, since all but Richard had passed out in the warehouse and awakened there. I duly wrote about all of it, the sale, the debauch, the fights, the fact that the next day our work continued. My charges were hardly voracious readers, yet there was little chance a column of mine would be overlooked by them, inasmuch as Johann, ever on the lookout for evidence against me, brought in a copy of the newspaper religiously each time a piece of mine appeared. The reaction on average approximated what it always was, a mix of sullen suspiciousness and sardonic sniping. Hermann offered up his critique that it was a three blowjob piece, a standard of criticism based on my charges' assumption that loose leftist women were everywhere waiting to reward me for writing what they wished to hear.

But Richard had disappeared. The day after our blowout

he was there, but the day after the column appeared, he was gone. I allowed for the possibility that he was ill, or that he was reevaluating and might yet return. The other boys didn't seem to know much about it. It turned out they weren't close to him. The three together were comrades, but Richard had been the stray dog. This I had more or less understood from the beginning, but not to the degree that they would think it good riddance if he was gone.

So I was the only one that was fond of him, and even me he pissed off. I went looking for him. I found him living with his mother in a cruelly colorless and dilapidated apartment block. The apartment stank of years of sour cooking. Richard invited me only a few feet in. He doubtless didn't wish the neighbors to hear us speaking; at the same time, the entrance hall to the apartment was so narrow that even his slender frame, when he backed away from the door a few steps, was enough to block any invasion I might have planned of his mother's reeking home. Richard wore his athletic jacket indoors. A recent haircut had made him look more skeletal than ever. Viewed from a certain teleological angle, he could have been an apprentice angel of death. I asked him where he'd been, an ill-designed question all but asking for a smartass, dumbshit answer.

"Right here," was all he said, in a shuffling monotone.

"We missed you. You're not coming back to work?"

"Why should I?"

"Well. It was what we agreed. It was what you committed to do."

"I don't anymore."

"I understand that."

"You said if anybody wanted to quit, they should just quit."

"But I wanted to know. We hadn't heard from you."

"What did you think?"

"I'll tell you what I thought," I said. My voice gained breath and certainty. "I thought even a little shit like yourself wouldn't leave without giving some kind of notice."

He nodded. But where I expected bitter words, all I got were his watery eyes. And they were the real surprise. I hadn't imagined that what they contained were tears.

He hung his head so that I couldn't see. "Why did you write that?" I heard him say, the words trickling up his nose, his forehead, the stubble of his hair, to my ears.

"Write what? Which part? I wrote about the party, I wrote about our selling the car…"

"All that. About me."

"What did I write about you? All I remember that I wrote about you is that you didn't really participate in our drunken brawl."

"You said I was queer."

"What? I did not. Of course I didn't."

"You might as well."

"By saying you didn't get drunk? By suggesting you might have had a feather's worth of good sense?"

"Jews think everyone's queer."

"Jesus. Come on. Richard."

"You can have my invention."

"Thank you very much. But it wasn't exactly something you could patent, you know."

"Then fuck off."

He was so skinny he looked deflated to me then. Or he could have been both skinny and deflated, all that was left of him was bones and sorrow.

"Come back. What shit. This is stupid," I said. Suddenly

it sounded to me like I was talking to a woman. The insane things you say to get her back.

But I did want Richard to come back, despite all my pronouncements about open doors. He had always been my favorite. He'd become like a mascot. And I hadn't even known it.

He shook his head, or it seemed to shake itself, like the head of a raggedy doll. He disappeared into the maw of the sour apartment. I waited longer than I would care to admit for him to change his mind.

In due course I conducted interviews and recruited a new fourth member for our crew. Günther was an efficient little savage whose specialties were carburetors and, as I later learned, harassing Africans on the U-Bahn. Skin Enterprises continued its mission of showing how the most discontented elements of the Eastern citizenry might yet be brought into the western settlement, and of course how a Jew could learn to love his enemies for fun and profit.

I wrote more columns about it all, especially when I realized the columns worked as advertising for the cars. But I never wrote a word, until now, about Richard, whom I found I continued to miss. It wasn't to protect him that I kept that silence. I may have been too successful in the love-thine-enemies area. I didn't want the world to think I was a wuss.

HOLLY ANHOLT

Boyfriend

I'LL SAY ONE THING more about Nils, mention one thing more, something he said the night we met, at Oksana and Herbert's party. It wasn't only his words but their jagged, discontinuous appearance, they connected so tenuously to our trite back-and-forth up till then that they must have been waiting there all along, a certain pressure building, like a chick ready to come out of its shell, ready-or-not-here-I-come. We'd been talking about my fleabag hotel, where as a reporter he'd once covered a murder. Nils said: "You know the dirty secret of every professional in Germany today? That if it wasn't for the mass murder of the Jews, half of us wouldn't have a job."

He said it very calmly, very conversationally, as if it were no big deal, as if he'd hardly changed the subject. Maybe he hadn't, really. Reporters, professions, his life, his career. Of course I didn't know what to say.

I caught his squint, then averted my glance, like a reluctant witness to a crime. My silence forced him to go on.

"And how many would give their job up, if the Jews could come back to life? It's what we call a competitive advantage, to be alive."

"Do you think about it?" I lamely asked, wanting to help, wanting to say anything at all.

He said: "You don't have to think about something when it's in the air you breathe. There are ghosts around. Ghost doctors and ghost lawyers and ghost professors and ghost businessmen and ghost editors and ghost artists and ghost actors and ghost biologists and chemists, and ghost reporters. All you have to do is dream about them."

And: "We can even ask ourselves, we German professionals and intellectuals and artists of the post-war: are we doing as good a job as those who are missing would have done? Or is it even possible, our consciences pricked, that we're doing a better job, or anyway a different job, or, heaven help us, a more German job?"

He was still in that conversational voice, steady, a little bit steely, as if at cost to him somewhere along the line he'd learned the secret of preserving emotion in the amber of facts.

So that's my story and I'm sticking to it, of how I became sure that Nils would be my boyfriend. Later, after I met his friend David, I pointed out to Nils that his best friend David was a journalist, and *he* was Jewish. "Precisely. My best friend in the world. But would I give him my job? That fat fuck?" Nils had a laugh like a crow sometimes, when he was really amused, and a triumphant snort could sneak through his sobriety.

NILS SCHREIBER

Girlfriend

ON MULACKSTRASSE IT LOOKED as if nobody had collected trash since the Wall fell. Empty lots like missing teeth, competing graffiti, foreigners out, Nazis out, on every exposed wall, and the faint traces of Yiddish over what had once been shop windows but were now as often as not boarded over. As midnight approached, a naked light bulb hung over a single open storefront. The storefront announced itself as an art gallery. In a spirit of bored curiosity, we entered. There were stairs and arrows leading to the basement. When we got down there, we had to walk over broken glass to get to the art, which was a dead rat suspended in the coal bin. Holly stifled what seemed like an unlikely scream. A girl with neon hair laconically held out a donation cup. I dropped a couple of marks in it. Holly wore flats with thin soles and was afraid she would cut her feet on the glass. The gallery was housed in the building her father had once owned, but her parents had never lived there and Holly showed little interest in this, her second claim. This was despite my suggestion that it might one day be worth a pile, that the old ghetto of the Scheunenviertel – centrally located, morbidly appealing, and left to rot during the GDR – was already showing signs of being Berlin's next neighborhood of the future.

FRANZ ROSEN

Hero

THIS IS A STORY ABOUT MYSELF. I was born into prosperous circumstances. My father owned an industrial firm which processed tungsten for the production of electric light bulbs. He was a confidant of Walter Rathenau, the assimilationist business leader who became the Weimar Republic's foreign minister in 1922 and was assassinated. When I was young, I led the life of a little prince. My elder brother was destined for the family business. I would be an artist, or a writer, or simply a dandy. My heroes were the assimilated Viennese writers with pens of quicksilver, Roth, Zweig, and (unfortunately if inevitably) for a certain period Weininger, who equated Jewishness with femininity and condemned them both. My father was neither a prophet about the Nazis nor a fool. When they came to power, he had the idea, I believe, of ducking down and muddling through: this too shall pass. A great believer in Germany's modernity, he perhaps underestimated fascism's appeal to that very modernity, a mistake in which of course he would not have been alone. My brother Paul was arrested and badly treated. On his release, he had sunken eyes. My father commenced considering emigration for us all. Paul was rearrested. This second time they sent him home in a box with his overcoat stuffed in. My father died of a broken heart. My mother suffered a nervous breakdown and the diagnosis of cancer virtually at once. It became too late to leave. We lost everything to confiscations. My mother was relocated to an overpopulated apartment in the ghetto of the *ostjuden*, where she promptly died, either from her cancer or the embarrassment of her new circumstances. I went underground in the city. My complexion and hair made me look sufficiently "Aryan." I had never quit attending the city's nightclubs, even after there were prohibitions. Now I made contact with other "U-Boaters," as we were called, Jews who lived as we could, and we formed a loose alliance. My self-proclaimed role in "the underground" was to use my familiarity with the demimonde to begin love affairs with German officers, and to glean information which I passed along an uncertain chain. My circumcision proved an inevitable problem. I had to be both deft and clever, and in one instance, to an SS man who conceived a true crush on me, I was forced finally to admit who I was and to depend on his love and mercy. When these came into question, or more specifically when he tried to convert me into a "snatcher" of other Jews, I murdered him and retired into the depths of the socialist neighborhoods. On the war's end, I met a camp survivor named Herbert Kaminski. Through Herbert, my deeds became known to the Americans. Soon they earned me modest honors, which were then magnified in the new West Germany's wish to find whatever saving graces it could in the disgraceful past and to put a distance from the rest. I became Herbert's right hand man in his expanding business ventures. At first this consisted of nothing more than collecting rents from whores and pimps. But Herbert had bigger things in mind. "Somebody will have to rebuild this city. It may as well be us, its human rubble." Of course we were all human rubble then, we Berliners, but Herbert considered us the rubble of the rubble. As money for reconstruction flowed in, our new construction company received its share and perhaps more. I had always been handy with figures, and now I abandoned my dreams of literature and became the one Herbert trusted with his numbers, his "Jew," as it were. My fortunes were restored. I imagined, despite my inversion, that my father would have been proud of me. I came to be considered a wise man in Berlin's miniscule remnant of a Jewish community. I became, at long last, a Zionist, and when the West German government established reparations funds to aid Israel, I was named trustee of one such fund. I turned ascetic as well. My dandy days gone, I donned a dark overcoat like my brother's in all sorts of weather. It was apparent that I was one of those whom the war had singled out to recast into an unlikely hero. I often spoke at those inspirational occasions held in Berlin's churches where the theme was "never again."

In addition, I wished to do my part to help my Israeli brothers find peace in their new land. I attended conferences and sent money. At one such conference on the question of refugees, my heart went out to a young Palestinian. He called me his rose. This may sound at once preposterously kitsch and obvious, but its very simplicity touched me. It was not so much the end of my asceticism as the beginning of a devotion. From the start I knew that Khalil could lie to me. He often did. Yet I was touched by his usual affection, by his periods of "making up," and by the dispossession he had suffered, both different from and similar to my own, as if we occupied two wings of a triptych separated by a middle that was dark and unintelligible. From the outset my Zionism had been tinctured by the old European dream of a Jewish state that would be a moral beacon to the world's nations. After the war in 1967, I was shocked that Israel did not promptly vacate the various territories it had occupied, and in particular by its claim to keep all of Jerusalem forever. A rift developed between my ideal Zionism and the reality, a rift which I could only partly paper over by remembering that I lived in "safety" in Germany. And so when the Gulf War began in '91 and Israel was under assault by Saddam's missiles and there were legitimate fears of gas attacks, I was already prepared to have my moral sense cleaved. Khalil plied me with reports that, despite Israeli denials, Jews were being issued gas masks while Palestinians in the occupied territories were not. "Thousands will die. It's what they want, to have no Palestinians left." Despite Khalil's hyperboles, the injustice rankled. The East German state had warehouses full of unused gas masks. Inasmuch as it could be imagined that Israel simply hadn't enough gas masks to go around, I initially tried to broker a deal whereby Israel would grant asylum to a certain high-ranking Stasi man who happened to be Jewish in exchange for the East German gas masks. "Two for one," I suggested. "You get the ability to live up to your moral responsibility *and* one newly minted Jew."

Israel refused. Khalil continued to goad me. I finally determined that it would only be just if I took one year's interest from the reparations fund of which I was trustee and with it purchased the East German gas masks for Palestinian use. I had no inkling when I did so that Khalil was playing a double game with me: even while he was urging me to act, he was informing a Berlin reporter of my every action. "For arms, asylum, that is the deal," "a million gas masks," "millions of marks." And so on. He hoped, in effect, to involve me, and Israel, and Israeli-German relations, in a dreadful scandal. He hoped to ruin me, or at the very least he didn't care if he did, if in the bargain he could harm Israel.

You may perhaps see the outlines of a morality tale here, or perhaps a tragic hero's fall. But I warned you at the outset that this was a story about myself. Perhaps, for greater warning, I should have put the word "story" in italics. The reason being that certain all-important portions of this story I've told – comforting received wisdom though they had become to many – are just that: a story. I am referring to my so-called "war record," my actions in an underground Jewish resistance in Berlin during the war, my heroic, or whatever you would say, murder of an SS officer. Lies. All lies. Or if you will, perhaps, the only genuinely literary act of Franz Rosen's career. I spent the war in cowering terror in a coal bin in Prenzlauer Berg, afraid in nearly equal parts of being exposed and being bombed. The only sex I had was with a haberdasher who owned the building. He was a Nazi for sure, but the only secret information he held was his sexuality. I suppose that my "underground" fantasy started with nothing more than the basement I found myself in. I could go no lower in life than I found myself, but I could fly on wings of imagination. Is it possible for a lie to begin in metaphor? I imagined the underground of which I would be a gallant queer part, I imagined each of my Nazi lovers and the secrets they would divulge, I imagined how I would kill when I had to. These were even fantasies that I elaborated in acts of love with the haberdasher, who excited my pity and contempt. And of course in the war's aftermath there were those with complementary desires, those who wished to believe in Jews in underground activities here – so it was a convenient lie as well. No one, finally, had the heart to check it out too carefully. I wish I could say that the war had made me a killer. But it had made me a liar.

And it had done one thing more: it had exposed to my unavoidable stare my sexuality. Previous to the war I had had sexual liaisons, but with women, prostitutes chiefly, apparently in order to prove to myself my masculinity, to overcome a terror of the vagina which at the time I took to be ordinary and inevitable. My first inklings that things might be otherwise came in my affection for my brother's friends, who were hearty, athletic types, exemplars, really, despite being Jewish, of the estheticized, sexualized public sphere which the Nazis created, in which bodies and athleticism were worshipped. But these secret affections led me nowhere. It took the coal bin in Prenzlauer Berg to make things clear to me. My haberdasher was a brute, but astute enough, in his sexual instincts if little else. He spoke to me often about the mistreatment of the Jews being taken too far, as if to remind me how lucky I was and to persuade me of his compassion on which I depended. That compassion, however, he extended only to certain sorts of Jews, the artistic, the philosophers, the heirs to Heine as it were, not to the stock exchange Jews whom he blamed for the troubles of all of us; these feelings being in truth not far from ones I'd felt myself when I was young. He was conscripted to the *Volkssturm* in February of the war's last year. I have no idea what became of him.

Now came the Gulf War and my betrayal of my trust and Khalil's betrayal of me and the entry into my life of Nils Schreiber, the reporter from our city's progressive daily to whom Khalil confided and who became my relentless Javert. I have nothing but favorable reviews to offer of Nils Schreiber. More in point, I fell in love with him, at an age when I had felt I was almost beyond that possibility. He seemed so superior to Khalil in every particular, moral, emotional, physical, even I would say his height, his eyes, his voice, that I began to wonder if I was seeing in myself some late-blooming racism. Not that I ever had the remotest hint of an affair with Nils Schreiber. He was surely an active and satisfied heterosexual, involved for a considerable period with a pretty American girl. Rather, I loved him at a distance which decreased while my love grew, as a fox might love an able hound. Finally he had all the pieces in place. He cornered me in a beach cottage in Sicily to which I had fled. I was not displeased to see him. Other than in social settings, it was the first time we had met. I complimented him on the many pieces of his which I had read with pleasure over the years. Many of these had dealt with his favorite issue and perhaps on occasion mine as well, the fate of the Jew in Germany. I offered him tea and a local liqueur, but he chose only the tea. We discussed also his friend David Fürst, who had the *chutzpah* – I suppose this is a not inappropriate use of that tired phrase – to have taken a coterie of rightwing hotheads under his wing. Only at length did we get down to the business which had brought Nils to me. He had his article and was ready to publish. I read it over while he sipped his tea. The details were correct as far as they went, which is to say, they showed no inkling of the lies of my "war record"; the entire tenor of the piece was rather of the hero of the Nazi-time who had a taken a fall from grace.

Now by this time events had rather mitigated my crime. To protect his own reputation, Herbert Kaminski had reimbursed the reparation fund for whatever shortfall was involved. Because the war was over so quickly, the gas masks themselves still sat in a Berlin warehouse. With currency fluctuations, they had actually increased modestly in value. I had earned the Fund in the neighborhood of five percent by my "speculation in commodities," and Herbert would be promptly repaid. Nils had discovered these facts, and they appeared in his article, but they did lead me to wonder what kind of scoop this reporter was left with.

"Does the piece have real news interest?" I asked, more out of a compulsive editorial motive than for self-protection.

"I think so," he said, his earnest gray eyes watching perhaps for my flinch. "The news interest is you. Your character. Why someone with a sterling reputation would risk all of it, even cheat, for a moral cause that nonetheless could be easily challenged."

"And your answer is…Khalil? But if that's the answer, I'm quite the dupe, am I not? It's what your article must inevitably imply."

"He does seem, let's say, unworthy of you."

"Well I assure you, Khalil has some very decent qualities. When he wishes to be, he can be warm and sincere. He appears to adore his new wife and family. He detests homosexuals, a fact which he's often conveyed to me, along with the assurance that he's not one himself."

"Then, why?"

"You see, Mr. Schreiber, I don't wish to be humiliated. I may deserve to be humiliated, and so that part of me, that recognizes my worthiness for it, of course demands it. But at the same time I wish to be saved from it."

"I don't follow."

"No. Of course."

"You wish me to humiliate you? But that's not the article's intention. It perhaps even shows you in a flattering light."

We were on my terrace, on a cloudy day, with a view to the gray sea. So far away from my only real home, I suddenly felt lucky to have been found, like a runaway who will soon be taken back to the rude shelter he has always known, and who feels, despite the cruelties he may have experienced there, that it is the one place that knows him well. I sipped my own tea and decided to tell Nils Schreiber: "More importantly, Mr. Schreiber…you see, I am a fraud. The great Franz Rosen, one of the fairies who slept with the Nazis for the underground… all false." I then supplied him with the various details, the coal bin, the haberdasher, my fear, my lies. "Now *that* would be a scoop, wouldn't it, Mr. Schreiber? To replace the one that fell rather flat? I suppose you'll be smart enough, I suppose I'll not have to connect every dot of my shame. But…a man may wish to act once in his life with the moral courage on which he's dined for forty years."

My words had their desired effect: tears in the gray eyes of this thoughtful man. It was as though, if you'll pardon me, the sea beyond us was reflected there.

At length I asked him if he thought, when his article appeared, that I could be charged with some sort of crime. He thought most certainly not. I insisted we drink to that, and got out a bottle of wine. He raised his glass but it was I who made something of a toast: "Be sure to write – I think this is good, perhaps – a small part of the guilt money the Germans gave the Jews, a Jew gave the Arabs. Or rather, tried to… You know when people are most easily made fools of, don't you? When they wish to be the hero."

SIMONA JASTROW

Confusion

WHEN I WAS BORN, and where I was born, divorce was rare. Nonetheless my parents seemed to manage it. It was the time of the yellow star and of being booted out of everywhere. You would have thought it was a time for sticking together. But no. I was too little at the time to understand all – I was nine – but what it seemed like, and from what they said, which was contradictory and not really to be believed, even by me, my mother wished to emigrate and my father didn't, then subsequently my father wished to emigrate but not with my mother. This emigration business never seemed the whole story. Then my father, who always talked about the Socialists, said to us that the Soviet Union was our only hope. My mother thought this was crazy. Later she would say it was his way to get rid of her. My father said *that* was crazy. He went to the Ukraine and worked on a collective farm. My mother obtained passage for her and myself to Shanghai. We had little money left but we made it. Our life in Shanghai was not at all full of the fun and games that some authors have described. Afterwards we emigrated to Vancouver, B.C., where my mother married a high school principal. I grew up and found Vancouver and all of it, my mother's life, our life, repulsively bourgeois. Shortly after the GDR's founding, I myself moved back to Berlin, convinced of the need to build Communism in the land of its invention. My father, I learned, had fought in the Red Army and survived the war. We resumed an occasional awkward communication by letter. He had other children by now and what I took, sight unseen, to be a shrewish, fat Russian wife.

My ardor for my new/old country was enhanced by being flattered. The fact that I'd come back from North America seemed to increase the stock that various higher-ups in the regime placed in me. I was installed on a journal. I was considered reliable. I was encouraged to write my own story. And in most aspects I was indeed reliable. I believed in equality. I believed we were besieged. I believed that Zionism was an inauthentic, doomed reaction to circumstances which late capitalism brought about and that West Germany exclusively, not the East at all, deserved to inherit the guilt for the war and the slaughter of all, Jews included. I was not blind to the seams of the GDR, but each time I observed them, I discounted, and explained, and recommitted myself. The hypocrisy could be discounted, for instance, by the supposed greater hypocrisy of the West. The corruption could be explained by the corrosive effects of the Western conspiracies to undermine us. The regime's harshness was necessary because our enemies were real and strong and ubiquitous, and only when they let up could we afford to relax our vigilance. I embraced such opinions until the end, that is, at which point, deprived of the lying, autocratic structures of authority which supported them, my beliefs – already straining, as I've indicated – collapsed utterly. This is not a flattering picture of myself, but it accurately describes the self-loathing around which my disillusionment wrapped itself. By 1991, I had been living for eight years at the East German Writers Union retreat in Velden am Moritzsee, not far from Potsdam. I was supposed finally to be putting to paper my autobiography, but I was paralyzed by my disillusionment. Why had I come to the GDR at all? My old explanations seemed as convenient and lying as everything else. By any account, it had been an unlikely journey. I felt the waste of my life. But who could I blame? It was then I met Electra Papaiannis, through the suggestion of a former colleague of mine in the Writers Union to whom I had confided my despair. Electra was a plump woman who favored loose clothing and heavy jewelry. She gave the immediate impression of being a Roma, which was of course reinforced the moment you learned of her profession. Electra conducted séances. Of course she was not a Roma, she was a Greek whose father had landed in a Düsseldorf restaurant decades previous. I had the vaguest ideas, from certain absurd films and articles, what a séance was. But I had lost both my parents in recent years, after decades of the faintest contact, and along with all else that had gone wrong, I missed them. Electra proposed to me that she might be able to help me. Now if you had told Simona Jastrow the devoted Socialist that a Greek woman in a shapeless dress could put her in touch with her dead parents, she might have written little notes to the proper people about all of you. But I was no longer that Simona Jastrow. I was Simona Jastrow who was devoted to nothing, who had nothing, who was lost. Here you see my vulnerability, here you see how doubters could attack me. But I freely admit it all. I had nothing to lose. This is when people do everything worthwhile in their lives.

There. At last it's done, or at least begun. The story of myself. My documentation. Mission accomplished, for the eager support the defunct Writers Union gave me over the years. You know what I say to all of it? Bullshit. You know what I really want to write about? I'll tell you what's really on my mind. I'd like to scratch out every word of my past. I know what other people say about me. I know all of it. Do you think I don't know? Of course I know. I've known all along. The one shining, perfect example: Anja Mann. She's confronted me with her hauteur. I told her, I said to her, to her face, I said, "Anja, at least I admit. At least I come clean. Everyone wrote notes about everyone else, and if they say otherwise, they lie." She says to me, "I never wrote notes." Not her, not the great Anja, the great civil rights leader, the taunter of Honecker and the rest. Bullshit. She probably did, in her sleep, with the sluts of the regime she slept with. I know these things. Why am I a leper, why am I maligned? Malign us all, but then shut up. Another perfectly good example: Oksana Kozlova. Top of the Red heap, *nomenklatura* through and through, now she comes around, she drives my new would-be landlord up to the house in her silver little shitty new Mercedes-Benz car, and what's she saying, what's she poisoning my new would-be landlord's ears with? I don't have to have been there to know. It was all in her knowing expression when she came to the door. "Oh, Simona, everyone knows Simona, *pure* Stasi!" What the hell does that mean, *pure* Stasi? She slanders me right in front of my new would-be landlord, tries to get me kicked out! I've lived here eight years. I'm the only one left. I told her, the would-be landlord, I tried to make it even a joke, so she'd understand, I'm from the States too, almost the States, so fuck it, so it's Canada, so what, Canada, I'm from North America too, so I say, "Simona Jastrow, Last of the Mohicans." And she didn't laugh, and you know why she didn't laugh? Because that cunt Red whore Oksana had already "told her all about me." Fuck her and all her progeny, if she didn't have too barren a womb to have any. And anyway it was true what I reported about Anja Mann, that she projected Zionist tendencies.

There. That feels better. Now I can resume. Where was I? Oh yes. Electra Papaiannis. The séances. Which those too, by the way, the likes of Anja Mann and all the rest would savage me for: "From ardent Communist to ardent communing with the dead, in what? Two snaps of a finger? Some people need faith badly." Fatuous self-righteous crap. She'll see, Anja will, the West has no need for her moralizing, her endless boring starch. I slept with her once. No fun at all. There. Forgive me. The séances, on the subject of the séances. I invited Electra to come to the Writers Guild house and organize them. Every other Tuesday night, twice a month. Get out the candles, darken the library, Electra's coming! They were the only moments of my weeks that I feared and looked forward to. Mama didn't come. Father didn't come. Nobody came for me, I had no idea what I was doing or supposed to be doing, I listened, I purified my mind, I invited celestial thoughts, I did whatever Electra said to do. And you know for the others, tables moved, whatever else, voices, trances. I thought they were insane and I wasn't. What a distraction it was from everything else. To have something, however absurd and unlikely, that offered hope, or as I might rather put it, still the possibility of beating life at its own game. This went on for two months, then the American arrived.

Was *chauffeured,* if you please, driven up by that little cunt Oksana in her whored-for car. Driven up like a princess out to do her shopping, "Ah yes, I'll take two of these and one of those, and don't *those* look delicious, and by the way I think I'll just have that nice house over there. What? There are already people in it? But look, I have papers, I have a claim! My, my, we'll just have to see about this. People already living in *my* house?"

Obviously, I get excited about this. You see, this house, this empty old GDR house, this empty institutional functionaries' house, had become my home. I had my room, I had my things, I had my curtains. My bedspread, even my bear. Yes, my bear, you admit you have a stuffed bear and people will think what a pathetic fool, what an insane one, who never lived past childhood! Well screw them, let them think whatever, I happen to know others who have a stuffed bear, I've heard, I've read, it's not so unusual, but even if it were, the point I am making is that even when the Writers Union retreat in Velden am Moritzsee later claimed by some American who never lived there a day in her life was empty of every writer but me, it was not the center of my universe but its entirety, that to which my universe had been reduced, where Electra with her brood of seekers came every other Tuesday night. I would serve them tea afterwards. Slowly I got to know a few of their names.

The American was the hugest distraction. After her first appearance with the Russian slut, she began to make regular visits, every two weeks, every week, looking around, imagining. Mrs. Baum would hear her coming in her cute little fixed-up car. Who did she think she was? These were always Mrs. Baum's words. More to the point, who did *we* think she was? She had a claim. We had no idea how long it might take to be processed or if it was valid. We had little idea of her intentions, because she never said. She was unfailingly polite and mild. She came and wandered around, in the house, in the fields, down to the lake. She was like a visitor from another planet. This, too, is what Mrs. Baum often said. And when and if she took over, would she dismiss the caretakers first?

And would her last living tenant last-of-the-Mohicans-Stasi-collaborationist-despised-by-all-for-her-honest-accounting-of-the-reality-of-how-things-were Simona Jastrow be given the boot as well? By all accounts, I should have been the first to go. It turned out my room was this Miss Anholt's parents' old bedroom. I let her in to look around. I imagined she hated everything that was mine. When she saw Bear-Bear, I cringed. Or perhaps it was she who cringed as well.

Obviously I tried to ingratiate myself with Miss Anholt. I brought her fresh local tomatoes. I showed her this and that around the house, ooh'd and aah'd at her old bits of film. My initiatives of course came with risks, in that she might have become more attached. At the same time I could imagine her thoughts, the nights she was at the top of the stairs while Electra conducted our proceedings in the library. I gleaned and wheedled. I tried to establish what her timetable was and her intentions. She had some boyfriend in the city, which for a certain period was a godsend, keeping her away most of the time. But inexorably her visits grew more frequent and longer, until it was clear to me that all my hopes that she would soon tire of us, or split with the boyfriend and so return to the States or Paris (or wherever it was she imagined she came from – really, it takes one nomad to spot another) were not to be realized. Finally I had it out with her. What else could I do? I accused her of many things. I told her how she had invaded us, how she had no thought for others, how she was a slave to little pieces of paper, money and deeds, how she could scarcely imagine how others' lives had been led, how limited she was, how small and pathetic, how everyone in Velden loathed her, how we knew perfectly well her plans to kick us out. Don't say that I went too far. I went as far as I needed to. She was taken aback. She admitted that yes, it was a possibility, that she would have to evict me. She claimed to have made no decisions, but I knew the truth.

And yet, from that confrontation, I grew to like the girl. She absorbed my attacks with bewilderment. She tried to explain her own quandary. For she had one, just like me. Something was hidden from her. She wasn't even certain what it was, except that it might be here, in this house or in the woods. She was very indefinite, and sad. I hugged her like a sister, and she hugged me back.

But now I had not a crutch left, not even my room with its pretty curtains and its view to the lake that I woke up to. My life here was over. My last defenses were down. Those whom I'd written little notes about haunted me and I woke up from nightmares begging their forgiveness. Surely this was too melodramatic, yet it created still another fault in me which I could not avoid. I put my things away, took them off the dresser, packed them up. My life felt over. I felt overwhelmed by my life's lovelessness. An endless waste, all of it. I wept and trembled.

Nor was it even any longer a pleasure or solace to recognize what cunts and monsters all the others were, those who would not even admit, even now, the comprehensiveness of our history's disgrace, so comprehensive it engulfed even themselves. I told Electra to call off her séances. I wanted nothing more with them. It had all been a fool's errand anyway. I had sat there in the dark befuddled. But she beguiled me. She wouldn't quite take my "no" to be final. She intimated that just then, when all hope was lost, when one's being had lost every structure of expectation and support, was when a miracle might occur. Though of course to her it was no miracle. To her it was all very scientific. The logic of the universe was called upon.

I gave in to her persuasions. I invited her and what I took to be her sorry band of followers for one last audition in the house. The procedures began, so banal I'm ashamed to write them, the hand-holding, the silence, the candles. When Electra channeled, her voice broke into a million pieces. She could have been anybody. I can recall that I stared at the bowl of oil that night and on this one occasion my mind did not flee to resentments or self-accusations or fantasies. My eyes seemed to slip into the bowl's oily substance, to swim in a place where vision is blurred. This is also absurd to write, is it not? Even now I can imagine my dear would-be landlord at the top of the stairs, listening in with condescension and confusion. What were these preposterous people doing in *her* house? And then, you can take this for true or not, you can tear it apart, you can ask what I *really* mean, you can believe your own fantasies about me, you can be fantastically cruel, whatever you wish, I cannot control it, be a cunt, go ahead, be my guest. But I became aware that both my parents were in the room, and that they were there together, it wasn't one of them on the left and the other on the right, avoiding each other's gazes and intimations, no, they were there together, as if hand in hand, they had reconciled.

How did I know this? You will of course want to know the gory details, whether I saw them with my eyes or heard them with my ears or through Electra's thousand voices or taps on the table or in a swoon, an ineffable sense, and was I like a saint struck down by God, a biblical story, what about a biblical story, that would make a nice story too. You'll want to have plenty of information to smash me with, to prove my impossibility. But I swear to you, and you can take it or leave it. My parents were there, and they were together, not hand in hand, I didn't see their hands holding one another, but it was *as if* they were hand in hand. Have you enough rope to hang me with yet? I expect little of the world, and from it least of all understanding. I felt their presence. And I knew that it was not a dream. It was entirely different from a dream. I felt their presence with a sense that I did not know I had.

I told my would-be landlord, she who would never get to boot me out now: "I'm leaving."

She was either surprised or relieved, but in any event she was speechless.

"I'm leaving Germany!" I said.

"Where are you going?" she asked.

"Jerusalem," I said.

"Well, that's a switch," she said.

"You know what happened? You know what my break-through was?"

She shook her head that she didn't know what it was. "Does it have something to do with your meetings, your…"

"You can say it! Séance! Séance! It's not a dirty word. Yes, of course!…My mother and father came!"

"To your séance? I thought your parents were…" Only then did it seem to occur to her that the entire point of a séance was for dead people to come. But I forgave my would-be landlord her dullness. I was too entranced. I was in love, I was at peace, I was overflowing with forgiveness. I wanted someone to know.

"And they were reconciled!" I cried. "They're together again. Do you know what that means? Do you know how long I've waited? Since I was a child!"

"They came *here*…two nights ago," she regurgitated with unhidden distress, which my intensity at once ran over.

"Listen to me. It all makes sense! After fifty years! Why I

came back, why I was such a stupid Communist! My mother and father divorced, yes, in 1937? Equals Germans and Jews divorced! In a young child's mind! What I never knew, never saw: that all I ever truly wanted from the GDR was a Germany that would reconcile Germans and Jews! Don't you see? The wish of a child for her mommy and daddy to be reconciled." I was exhausted by then. My voice dropped off to nothing. "Holly, they were in the room. My dead mother and my dead father…"

I wept gladly and, as she held me, I repeated: "It all makes sense, it all makes perfect sense." I knew then that I had made a convert, that my would-be landlord had begun to admit to herself that it made as much sense as anything else.

I have memorialized the conversation above because it is the only time I ever spoke out loud the truth that had overcome me. I invited Electra Papaiannis to conduct more séances in the house. I was hoping to see my parents again, to strike up a more natural, informal conversation with them, to learn more, to fill in details, to swap stories. This was a foolish hope. Of course they would not come again. But what was truly foolish about it was that I already had perfection. My mind was relieved. I had what I needed. I called off the séances. I packed up the remaining bits and pieces of my life. I took down my lovely curtains. Next year in Jerusalem became my motto.

HOLLY ANHOLT

Tenant

IT'S SO THAT I HAD BEEN WARNED by Oksana about Simona Jastrow. I took care right from the start with her. It's the case that, combined with suspicions I could scarcely avoid about myself for having made my deal with the Schiessls, Simona's presence in my parents' old house seemed to me a cruel omen. She was obviously obsessive, demanding, self-deluded, narcissistic, and mistrustful, the kind of person you could try to win over and be left with nothing but sand in your smile. So why did I come to pity her? I suppose for all those reasons. Or what I could finally see was her intelligence. Simona was right about something: that every person's politics are so deeply mixed with the personal that terrible mix-ups between them can take place. That the divorce of individuals could be confused with the divorce of peoples seemed as plausible as it was terrible.

As for the odd coincidence that she had once informed on my lawyer Anja to the Stasi, I knew it because Oksana had told me even when Anja had not. As between myself and Anja, and myself and Simona, it had to remain a secret. I didn't wish Simona to have another reason to mistrust me.

DAVID FÜRST

Tease

I AM UNFORTUNATELY AWARE of my own worst traits. I am a bully and I am a tease. Ask the American girl, ask Nils' friend. Of course her vulnerability, her naïveté, disturbed me. Jews aren't supposed to be so naïve. That's what comes from living in a country where you're hardly oppressed.

Yet what a delightful conversation I had with her in the back room of the Café Charlie. Johann and Heinrich were my witnesses, as I had brought them there to show them a bit more of all they had hitherto missed in life and might aspire to, techno girls and Gauloise smoke.

Holly had come in with Nils, but he was off on the phone, once more in pursuit of Franz Rosen, his great whale.

"And how are we doing on our psychotherapeutic ramble through the GDR countryside?" I asked good-naturedly. "Experiencing any epiphanies this week? Any *crise?*" I would not have been so facetious with her, but I was at a loss as to what else to say. Really, I was only trying to make conversation.

"Would you stop being such an asshole," she replied, also good-naturedly, a response clever enough that I translated for my boys, who were suitably impressed with the ability of Western girls to curse.

"So what's next? A little *tour de Pologne*, perhaps, for spice?" I asked.

"What are you talking about?" she asked.

"Auschwitz," I replied. "No tourist of shame would want to miss that. Psychodrama guaranteed, the past rising up like a puff of smoke."

"I can't believe you think you're being witty. Have you even been to Auschwitz?"

"Yes I have. When I was two."

So I scored my cheap points. Nils returned and the conversation moved on, to the fate of his story on Franz Rosen, or the very survival of our old paper in the new penurious, post-unification era, or things of that nature. The West's realization that it no longer had to support us like little kings. Holly stayed grumpy with me then, offering no more than a pout and a bout of silence – and not without justification, I would add. But later I came to believe that I had put the idea of Auschwitz in her head.

OKSANA KOSLOVA

Father

WHAT WAS MY FATHER DOING on his trade missions to Switzerland? The official Soviet version was that he had been granted the privilege to travel abroad in order to negotiate gas contracts. Unofficial versions inevitably had it that these gas contracts were only a cover – no more than a piddling few were said to have ever been completed – and that the real reason for the trips was, variously, to make hard currency deposits on behalf of the Party in Swiss accounts, to make such deposits on behalf of individual high-ranking members of the Party in such accounts, or to invest the Party officials' money in American securities. All these versions allowed for a juicy conclusion: my father had the opportunity to steal. And so gossip, or as it may have presented itself, character analysis, came as accompanying baggage. I learned that my father, who had always brought me very nice gifts from the West, was a swindler, a confidence man, a charmer, a womanizer, and for the icing on the cake, a Jew. It was then inevitable for the character analysts to conclude that he had been caught absconding and paid for his crimes with his life. But if so, where was the body? The Swiss were said to be orderly people. Was the body at the bottom of Lake Geneva?

You can therefore imagine how I held out hope. I dreamed

of my father in various exotic settings, in Monte Carlo or Las Vegas, gambling the Party's money away, having a high time of life, and thinking every once in a while of me, and of the present he would send me home.

No present ever came. Years passed; my mother's flight to Finland with a man; my esteemed grandfather's guardianship over me. A girl grows up. I slept with Mischa Lander once, the hardly publicity-shy German spy, in the understanding that if there was anything in the Stasi records about my father, he would tell me. He told me there was nothing, and he must surely have been telling the truth, because he knew that if there had been anything there, I would have slept with him again.

There are still days when I imagine that some present might arrive, or that I might run into my father, unslept and unshaved, in a park or on the U-Bahn of any Western city you can name.

MISCHA LANDER

Exile

KINDLY CONSIDER THE UNFAIRNESS of the situation. I have conducted my life in a way that was both lawful and helpful. Lawful according to the laws of the society in which I lived and helpful to the world as a whole. Oh yes, you would deny this? Someone on this earth has to stick up for the poor. That is of course what it was all about. No one can finally deny this, even as they peck at all the rest of our entrails. If you help the poor, you had better win. But it's not so easy to win such a battle.

And for my troubles, now even Israel denies me entry. They let every Jewish gangster in, they even let Meyer Lansky in. Why? Because they have no choice, they say, he's a Jew, so they let him in. It's the law, they say, the right of return, all of that. But when it comes to Mischa Lander, oh no, wasn't he high up in the Stasi, we'll see, we'll have to see. When he's dead, that's when we'll decide. Politics seem to extend even to who is a Jew. Well, very well. It's what I always thought.

Regardless of what you have been taught, it is not only in the East that show trials have their place. Germany would delight to see me in the dock. So I have pulled what levers I can. All have been worthless. When your country disappears, so self-evidently does your leverage. I had hoped nonetheless to conclude a fair bargain: a prominent Zionist wished Israel to obtain a supply of GDR gasmasks which it might still have been within my power to obtain. All I asked in return was that they accept me in the bargain, which even this Israel refused.

I am only a little embarrassed to say that I am now reduced to what some would call, rather imprecisely, blackmail. I know a few things about the worthy businessman Herbert Kaminski and a few things about his Russian wife and a few things more about Kaminski's lieutenant, who is precisely the prominent Zionist with whom I previously negotiated. What makes the situation the more delicate is that I am rather fond of the Russian wife. Oksana Koslova calculates as I do. It's as though we went to the same school.

I continue to be appalled that Israel would take a man who has been portrayed even in films as the greatest gangster of them all and will not take me. The country lacks the spirit of universal brotherhood. Yet I am not surprised.

OKSANA KOSLOVA

Students

NINA ORLOVA HAD THE PALEST, thinnest face and hoped to apprentice to a haircutter. Gregory Rakuzin had been an engineer in Irkutsk but he came with his wife and two children and so was driving a taxi seven shifts a week. Maria Volozova could have been only eighteen and every bit of German grammar baffled her but she wished, she said, to become a teacher like me. Ilia Fet worked three jobs and was saving to bring his family and when they were all situated he would work even more jobs and then open a video shop on the Kantstrasse. Raisa Goldshtein was in her thirties, her hair was jet-black and straight, she was talkative and rather loud and made no bones of her aspiration to one day run the finest escort service in Berlin. Sasha Tabachinksy would learn German because he had to but he would write his novels in Russian. There were others as well. I can hardly describe, do justice, to the hopefulness of these people. It was on their faces every minute, in their schemes and deductions. It suffused their efforts. They looked at me as if I were the key to some kingdom they could clearly imagine but not quite grasp. But soon they would, of course I presumed they would, they would figure it out and everything would be fine and they would write home to whoever was still there about their success.

But first they would look at me with hope.

You may suppose how disturbing this was, to be looked at in such a manner every day of the week. It came to seem like an accusation against me. Among other things, why was I even working here? A volunteer, no less, as if I were already taking on the protective coloration of a rich woman. Why wasn't I home painting? Why was I giving back to my tribe and was this even what it was?

I adored those faces of my students. There were even days when I went home and tried to paint them, but I couldn't capture their desire, as I had too little of my own. After three months at the émigré center, I quit. They begged me not to. They must have thought I was competent, or some such. But their begging only served in my mind to increase the unrecoverable distance between us. If I could have traded my life for any one of theirs, I would have.

HOLLY ANHOLT

Journey

NILS THOUGHT IT WAS A BAD IDEA. He'd been there himself, so his skepticism could be taken two ways, either the considered voice of experience or the light condescension of someone who thinks something's right for him but not for you. I decided to take his advice both ways. I'd go, but with appropriate fear, doubt, and self-loathing. He would have gone with me but he was in the Middle East covering the Gulf War. I would have waited for him to return but I thought, no, I'm a big girl, I have a car, I have my plans, I should carry them out.

Nor was Nils the only dissenting voice. Oksana furrowed her brow and of course David mocked me for it. "A little *tour de Pologne*?" One more of his little phrases. "It's in the papers. American woman seeking enlightenment. No job too dirty." But then, David was always mocking me. Nils' best pal had so successfully taken on the relentless aspect of my nemesis from fifth grade that I had begun thinking of ways to mollify him, which, as I'm sure he understood, is how I wound up buying one of his cars. The customer's always right: wasn't he teaching his charges capitalist tricks? But David was the worst capitalist I ever met.

I stayed the first night in Cracow. I won't bore you with the guidebook descriptions. It seemed alright, it was old, it was no longer Communist. One more "Paris of the East", or something else of the East. I stayed in a place called the Metropole that was still musty and chintzy from the old regime and the next day drove to Auschwitz. You know there are signs for it on the motorway, Oswiecim, this exit. I found that rather odd. But then, it's a good-sized town. You couldn't not have signs for it. I began to feel badly for people who were born there. If they ever went anywhere, they'd have so much explaining to do. Or maybe they never went anywhere, just for that reason. Or maybe they just never went anywhere period. I was afraid and thought about such things.

I can't remember how you get from the motorway to the main camp. There must have been signs but I don't remember. The main camp is the one with the "Arbeit macht frei" sign and the museum, but it wasn't actually the extermination camp. The approach is by a cobbled path that could have been to a zoo or a monastery, and the buildings themselves are of brick and neat enough. There was plenty of room in the parking lot. It wasn't a very popular place in the autumn of 1991. I walked the cobbled paths, like a proper museum-goer read the guide and observed the displays. Everything was stacked high as if you were getting something wholesale, empty suitcases, pairs of shoes, Zyklon B cans, hair. Now *there* would be a punishment, a just retribution, to have to spend your life counting up every single human hair, and if you make one mistake, if you miss one hair, you have to start over. I thought such things. I was alone. And this too: if work can't make you free, what can? Only God's grace? Only love? Only luck?

I left, feeling properly alienated, as if this wasn't what I'd come for, this main camp with its straight paths and brick buildings and numbers on the buildings that could have been a second-rate prep school or what in fact it once had been, a Polish army barracks that the Nazis grabbed. If I was making a pilgrimage at all, it had to be to the other camp, the outlier, Birkenau, Auschwitz-Birkenau, Auschwitz II, the processing plant of death. I drove the couple miles and parked in a muddy lot. Now this was more like it, out of town and out of the way, vast, dilapidated, destroyed and gray; I laced on boots and looked up at what I'd seen in pictures, the watch tower with its fort-like flanks extending in either direction and the hole in the wall in the middle where the trains went through. There was only one other car in the parking lot, Polish or Russian and rusted out. I'm not even sure how I knew that this *was* the parking lot. But there weren't any other cars anywhere else. It seemed like it would rain soon.

There was a guard house to one side of the portal. I entered, to see if I needed a ticket. A wasted-looking kid about eighteen in a green shirt thrust a guest book at me. I signed without even looking at who had signed before me. The kid pointed to a stairs and said in English, "Go! Up! You see whole thing!" I said, "Thank you, not now," or whatever I said, and the kid retreated to a second room where another kid in a green shirt was waiting for him, with a couple of glasses and a vodka bottle. One of them slammed the door shut. Immediately a radio went on, the music loud and laced with acid. I filched a small map off a pile of them, left the guard house, and walked through the portal, hearing from inside the sounds of falling-down drunkenness, shouts, the music, static, people or things crashing into walls. I can remember thinking: they weren't expecting anyone today.

By now, I don't really know but I imagine, there's a bit of an Auschwitz tourist industry, the buses filling the muddy fields, or who knows, there could be a paved lot by now; but that cloud-laden afternoon, it was just me and the two Polish guards; and I soon forgot their drunken brawling or dancing or whatever it was.

In my numbness, I forgot pretty much everything, even why I came. I could observe but not feel. This of course I recognized as possibly emblematic of my life, but it didn't make it any easier. How much I wanted to have definitive reactions, to make connection, to truly be where I was. But as I walked down the weedy railroad track, looking back every once in a while at the "Portal of Death," I was more like those drunk guards. If I'd thought about them then, I would have understood them.

On each side of me, past barbed wire, were low wooden barracks, like sheds, that went on tirelessly in rows, and where the barracks left off, there were chimneys where the burnt ones had been. And why was the barbed wire still there, why had no one ever bothered to remove it? Evidence, all was evidence. That's how someone must have thought about it. And of course they'd have been right. Such old barbed wire. There was a break in it and I went through to the sheds. The little map I'd grabbed in the guard house said these were the women's barracks. I looked through cobwebbed windows, uncertain what I was seeing. A creaking door flapped open and shut. I walked through it with superstitious dread, afraid something rabid might jump out and bite me. I can say only the few words my map said about the lines of hard bunks, that women slept head to toe, eight to a bunk, the bunks themselves stacked three high. Don't take my word for it. I won't vouch for such things. There were a few graffiti on the walls. Why should I have a preference if they were made by inmates or tourists?

All the same, all the same, the world is all the same. These were my thoughts. I was alone. Look here, a wash basin. Look there, a latrine. Back out in the open, I followed my map to where one of the gas chambers had been. A couple of steps to the undressing room remained. An indented, grassy spot that had been a pond of ashes.

Why I went back to the guard house is unclear to me. Perhaps I did want to see "the whole thing," as advertised. Perhaps I only wanted to see another human being. Only one of the bleary-eyed young men was there when I returned. He was the one I'd spoken with before. "Good?" That was what he asked me. "Good?"

He looked like a caricature, as well, half-steady on his feet with a cockeyed grin, as if the noise I'd heard before was him bouncing himself off the walls.

"Oh, very good. Very good. The only not good thing, if you want me to be critical, was it wasn't horrible enough."

"You want go up? See whole thing. Very good." His old refrain. He threw an arm towards the stairs.

And probably because I'd been sarcastic and regretted it, I gave in to his persistence. Maybe he was right, maybe it was something I should be seeing. I nodded and followed him up the narrow stairs, oddly aware of the mud on my boots, as if I were tracking mud into someone's house.

The upstairs space – you could hardly call it a room, it was more like a narrow attic – was fetid the way you'd expect if it was the retreat of these boys. Odd, too, but I felt no fear going up there, as if once you're afraid of everything, it's hard to be afraid of anything, there's no longer background to tell the foreground. I looked out through the wind-filthy window at "the whole thing." I tried, without success, to imagine what my parents must have done to survive this place. The field of play below me had become familiar. Death, but at a suitable distance. I again began to compose such thoughts, to become lost in my opinions or what I would someday say. To Nils, for instance, what I would say to Nils. Though he was hardly a "for instance," there was no one else to tell, my mother being gone. Dearest Mother, Dearest Father, what? This was not the place I would remember them or know them, this was only a long gray field where it had begun to rain. Then I felt the boy behind me. His breath stank of vodka and garlic.

"Love me? You want love?"

I could feel his chest and legs on me. I turned, to laugh him off or push him away.

"No. Are you crazy?"

He put his hands on me and with a Brueghel leer tried to kiss me.

I'm not sure what then happened first or second but he kept talking about love, nice love, have nice love, American girls like love, in that ridiculous stewed pidgin, then we were wrestling and I wrestled him away and the stairs seemed far away. For certain he grabbed my breasts and I spit on him and we wrestled on the filthy floor. He got a knee between my legs and fumbled with his pants. I screamed whatever I screamed. I was as tall as he was but he was stronger. Everything was disjointed. The only thing I remember clearly thinking is what if the other one came back, if the other one came back then I'd be done for, because what would they do, they'd lose their jobs, they'd have to kill me and I'd be the only Anholt to die in Auschwitz.

But the other one didn't come back. Nor did the first one rape me. I don't know how long we wrestled or exactly which body parts of mine he touched. What I thought at the time was that I freed myself by desperate effort, that I somehow rolled away and pulled my leg away from his reach and made the stairs and he didn't follow me down. But the truth is he may have spent himself in his pants. In retrospect, later in the Metropole in the so-called light of day, I decided I had heard a little groan.

My car suffered greater physical injuries than I did. When I woke the next morning, somebody had stolen the side view mirror, both windshield wipers, and the front grille. If it had been the grille from Oksana's Mercedes-Benz, I might have understood, but off my funny little clown car that barely made the trip, it was only adding ludicrous insult to injury. I laughed out loud then, thanking God for everyday life.

So much for my *tour de Pologne*. They won't be writing this one up in a tourist brochure. Driving home I thought, they ought to abolish all ruins, because they're phony, but they ought to keep the guards, because at least they know what they want.

I took care not to tell David of my misadventures. To Nils I told everything. He seemed to think it was his fault.

NILS SCHREIBER

Words

THINGS WHICH I SAID TO HER, at one time or another, whether they were true or not:

That we Berliners erect plaques so as to sleep better at night.

She had agreed to meet me for coffee and a walk. We were standing in Grosse Hamburger Strasse by Boltanski's memorial to the bombed-out and disappeared, on the block of the Jewish old age home that had been the roundup point for deportation. It was a cold, miserable October night, the uncollected detritus of the Scheunenviertel streets swirling around us like an early, dirty snow. Holly kept her silence. She dutifully looked. "We have a talent for memorializing," I also said, to fill the silence.

A wise guy, me, who could have said much more as well, could have opined with mordant proficiency on the substitution of monuments for active memory as it affects our personal lives, how we build our mental memorials, we change our furniture entirely around, one day it's this, the next day it's that, and still there's no forgetting, but only instead the transformation of feeling into stone. Or I might have confessed the twinge of bitter pleasure I might or might not have experienced in showing a visitor this neighborhood of mine.

Instead all I said was that I lived up the street.

She was taking no bait that night. She nodded and that was all. I thought she should speak, I wanted her to speak, to condemn my irony. But she already knew too much about me.

Later we walked the few blocks to where her father had owned the building that was now already an art gallery and was the subject of Holly's second claim.

That Miss Anholt, property claimant, was no longer the object of my journalistic intentions.

We were in bed and only half-dressed. She pounded my chest in mock anger, but her surprise was real enough. "You were going to write a story about me?" she cried like a shot bird.

I don't often laugh as I laughed then. "This is not only a confession, it's a promise."

"Oh thank you very much. How generous you are! How thoughtful!"

My words stumbled over my laughter. "Sounded good to me. American girl, totally American, post-war, nothing bitter, nothing more than curiosity, comes with a claim…just follow where it leads."

"And I bet I know why you're not writing it. Your editor doesn't want it! 'Too many stories with Jews, Schreiber. Don't you have anything else to write about?'"

"As a matter of fact…"

"I'm right! I'm right, aren't I? I'm right!" she repeated, pounding on me till we were ready to make love. "Bastard! Asshole!"

We may have known little more about each other then, but we knew we were joined in conspiracy. To be specific, I believe:

a conspiracy of guilt. Kissing, touching each other's nose and neck and hair. Things to remember, tenderness never to forget.

That dear Mother was in the cheerleading squad.

The B.D.M, the *Bund Deutscher Mädel*, the Nazis' girls. This I informed her of in my parents' bedroom, which for some reason we had entered, to get some piece of luggage down or something, over the Christmas holiday when we visited. Why I went along with this trip, or even subtly planted the seeds for it, is another matter again. The invitation was there. I hadn't been home in years. They had gotten word of the girl and presumably were curious. Holly wanted to, eager, as ever, to see whatever could be seen about me. I must have been mad. Perhaps I thought of it as a personalization of my great theme, the return of the living. Because why, because the killers are gone? Because the world is full of killers? Why do they come back?

Actually, Holly had been quite specific on the question of Christmas. She knew that I thought the idea was preposterous. Holly asked "what if?" We discussed such various "what if's." And in the end she half-expressed and half-confessed a sentimental attachment to an old record cover of her father's, a Brahms second symphony, that showed a steepled German church in the still, pale light of Christmas Eve. In a sense she wished to test this fantasy, to see if the life on her father's record cover could actually be lived.

This led, perhaps inevitably, to our overnight stay in a little inn in Oxenburg, near Hamburg, and to my mother's dresser. There were other photographs there as well, my father's retirement, anniversaries, their vacations to Spain and Rio de

Janeiro, my *gymnasium* graduation photo, portrait of a long-haired beanpole in black. Holly begged to differ. She saw an intense young scholar with the world in his dark sights. But when she was done cooing about her boyfriend, there was the small, creased snapshot of Gerhilde, long-legged and athletic, in hiking shorts, turning away for a moment from whatever mountain path she was on to have her moment in history taken in black-and-white. "How beautiful your mother looks, how happy," Holly said.

I told her about the B.D.M. She already knew my parents had been in the Party. But this image of youth, and happiness, and health, alarmed her. Her eyes tightened. She may have been envious. I was flooded with remorse. I wished to tell her everything she had that my mother had never had.

She stared at the picture a moment too long. "Your mother looked great in shorts," she said.

My parents, I should add, were as gracious as they could be during our day and a half in Oxenburg. My father was hearty and jocular and my mother baked without stopping for breath. They presented us with calfskin gloves. And they still looked quite fantastic, as if they climbed a mountain every weekend. Hartmut went on about his hero, Moishe Dayan, for whose benefit we'll leave to the reader to imagine. My mother kept her hectoring of my father to a minimum. I remained embarrassed and reluctant. Holly smiled at whatever either of them said. For certain she was struggling to see how I resembled them. My father's jocularity occasionally had a bit of an edge: "Just don't take him off to America! He's the only one we've got!"

And, on a point of interior decoration, not previously thought to be my long suit: I had never been so aware how stuffed with bric-a-brac my parents' middle-class house was. *Tchotchkes*, to use the proper Yiddish.

In the evening we went to church. A properly-steepled, eighteenth century church, by the way. Holly at least had been to a wedding or two over the years whereas I hadn't been in a church in my adult life, unless it was to cover a peace demo or a lunatic fringe. To keep her company, I pretended not to remember what to do, and was so successful at this that I actually began to be unsure. We stood when others stood, sat down when they sat down. Once we were caught half-standing when the congregation was merely reaching for its hymnals, but at least we were caught together. I couldn't tell a thing of what she was thinking, except by the music she seemed entranced.

We were up late that night in the inn, quietly, with the lights out. Holly couldn't sleep. She felt, she said, like a stranger to herself. "It started sometime in the carols. I thought: listen, Holly. Really try to listen. These lovely voices of children: are they singing to me with Christian love? Is this the reality Jews are blind to, that could convert a soul on the spot? I must be weak, I thought. I hear the lovely voices of children, and then…all I could hear was a lot of my own voice, like static. Telling me to listen. All these words. The music! I wanted to live in the music. But just then I couldn't.

"And so then I thought: is their love really different from mine? If they only knew how much a part of me wanted to be them, how that would simplify my life. To be converted to love and grace, me who just then was afraid I was living without either."

"Love is love," I said.

"Of course love is love," she said.

I kissed her the way you do when you wish to change a

lover's hurtful subject. But she was having none of it. Light-headed now, nostalgic to the point where her voice got frail and insistent, as if she had to will it to keep it going, she said, "Remember that record I told you about, with the church and Christmas Eve and the steeple and snow? Do you remember that, Nils?"

I said that I did.

"It was a cheap record. It was so cheap it had a hole punched through the label, to show it had been dumped by a warehouse or something. Probably a dollar apiece, but my father would buy piles of those records, until he had his classical collection complete, one or two of everything. Of course they weren't usually the star conductors, I don't remember many von Kara-jans. But they were good, always good, mostly guys he remem-bered from Europe… And they were a bargain, they were what he could afford, or thought he ought to afford… It gave him such pleasure. The size. The completeness. The economy. All a reflection of him, of the way he'd learned how to live."

She leaned closer to me, against my arm. "My father," she said.

Her eyes were lightly shut. Mine were wide open.

I thought of my own father and wished I had not.

That I slept with Oksana.

Well, it was so. I could hardly deny it. Or I suppose I might have, but this would not have been my style. Anyway, it was well in the past.

Still, Holly was not quite amused. She accused me of having a thing about Jewish girls. We had one of those conversations, sweet and hurt and silly all at once.

"I'll make a list for you of my lovers."

"Good. Then as I meet them I can check them off…"

About the Jewish girls, I denied. It's only good form to deny such things, to refuse to admit such paralyzing generalities. "How will you tell us apart?" she said. "Will you keep a score-card? Will you give us numbers instead of names?"

She thought Oksana must still be in love with me. She thought, when we were in Italy, that Oksana was bringing Herbert's files to me. But I knew otherwise.

As for the numbers, in the end I conceded her point. Perhaps I was more sociologist than lover. Numbers might make more sense. Number one was in New York and played the cello and showed me the whisper chamber in the basement of the train station there and had a neck as thick as a boy's but a gentle way that could seem a little defeated, that could make you root for her in fear. Number two was passing through. The same with number three, as best I could tell. Number four reminded me of my mother, an amazing thing considering my mother's coldness, sentimentality, narrowness, and preference for long, bracing walks over thought. Number five was the aforementioned skinny Russian girl. Number six was Holly. I took to calling her Number Six. She hated that.

But, of course, she was a sociologist too.

FRANZ ROSEN

Weakness

MY GREATEST FEAR was that I was careless of Herbert's reputation. You can say he should not have cared so much for what others thought of him, for his reputation in the city. But it was something he had earned, this reputation, it was something he had had to struggle for. All men are weak somewhere. Herbert's weakness was this, that he wished to be, if not loved, then respected. But really he wished to be loved.

I might say all of the same about myself, of course.

When I proffered my resignation, Herbert gave me money to make my escape.

OKSANA KOSLOVA

Separation

GO BACK. Turn around. Spool the film in the other direction. Something to make me smile. When I was a little girl, my mother held my hand. She put me in a fine coat and I squinted at the camera, in the Moscow sunlight, holding her hand.

NILS SCHREIBER

Words (Continued)

MORE THAT I SAID TO HER, at one time or another, whether it was true or not:

That I still found her attractive.

We were in Italy then and had not made love in a couple of days.

But there was nothing about her that was not attractive. She had a mild, honest sense about herself, she could see through things if she had to, her words were simple but accurate, she was slow to put her troubles on others, her eyes were large and dark, her smile was easy, she could be funny if really forced to be, she found the world interesting, she could hold onto a question until she wrung its neck or it wrung hers, she was not too proud, her legs were long and her ankles just slender enough, everything about her, truly, was just enough, she could run if she had to, she could do most things if she had to, she was not averse to a bit of lazing around, she was not averse to the bed, she was not averse to a good argument, her lower lip in particular was sensual, her thirst for revenge was small, she woke up in the morning with things on her mind, her breasts would kindle an Arab poet, she wore clothes in an offhanded way, she wasn't boyish at all, she seemed to possess a well of mercy, she was no more lost than I was.

Or I mustn't be flippant: she recognized, I recognized, we both did, I think from the very first, that a part of each of us was a little bit lost. A certain equivalence in this regard made our affair possible.

It was afternoon in our darkened room and I was reading. "Put your book down, Nils," she said. "I need to ask you something. Don't answer right away, okay, don't just assume an answer. Do you still find me attractive?"

"You asked me that question awhile ago," I said.

"No I didn't. I asked if you found me attractive. But then I decided you did. But now I'm wondering if you still do."

"I still do."

"But you're kind of aloof."

"It's only been a couple days," I said.

"So you are. That's how you feel."

I recovered the semblance of my slightly haunted smile and kissed her. We kissed two or three times more. She must have sensed something, the pressure of my lips, as slightly forced or willed. "Never mind. Go back to your book. Screw you," she said. "You're not doing me a favor, Nils. You're not favoring me with your presence!"

"Sorry. But I don't know what you want."

"Nothing. Never mind. I know, I'm just making trouble."

She grabbed a magazine off the floor and appeared to plunge into it, refusing to put it aside even when she realized it was in Italian and she could read hardly a word. There were not any pictures, either. This, too, I found attractive.

That I didn't care to instrumentalize her.

It was part of the same conversation and it could have been true or false. It was later and she had grown quiet. She had gone to the window and pulled aside a corner of the curtain. A shaft of sunlight illuminated her forlorn expression. Wherever it was that her eyes wished to take her, I could see that her mind was not. I was not to my knowledge a sadomasochist. No woman had ever whipped me or tied me up. I actually thought such things comical. But as I observed Holly's sad distraction in the harsh glare that streamed from the parted curtain, I saw, or I must have thought I saw, as in a negative, her anger.

"In a sexual sense," I added, when her incomprehension was plain.

She dropped the curtain and we were in the dark. But her voice was tender. "How do you know I don't want to be your instrument in a sexual sense?"

"Nobody wants to be a slave. Or if they do, I won't give them the satisfaction."

"What are you talking about, Nils? Who are you talking about?"

She'd come closer to where I was, on the low, thin mattress. "You, Holly," I said.

I was, as I thought, in the throes of the discovery of a kind of hope. I was throwing off my aloofness. These things I didn't say, as I didn't wish to embarrass myself.

"Nils, you can't make me your slave. I don't think so anyway. But I do want to be close to you," she said.

"You can't. You're far away."

"Don't say that."

"Because of your anger, you're far away."

"Don't make me afraid."

"Cut me," I said. "Hurt me. Make me bleed."

"What?"

"With your fingers, with your anger."

We were silent then. I could begin to see her again, sitting at the bed's edge, looming over me. A dark angel, her eyes glistened.

For a moment our eyes met, as she lifted my shirt away and placed her hands on my sides. "I'm not begging you, Holly," I said. And she, who had been commanded very little in her life, responded as though to a command. With no discernable erotic intention, rather with obedient deliberation, she spread my arms then squeezed my flesh with her nails. I could smell the blood when I was cut. "How could you not be angry with me? How could you not? Here's your chance," I said, and she drew her nails down my chest.

Later she would say that my face was such a picture of pain as she had never seen. But I felt no pain. "Holly," I whispered, "Where is your anger, Holly? Why are you lying? What are you hiding?"

When she struck me, it was with such a rush of anger that she screamed and struck me many times again.

That I didn't wish to give my native land another chance with a Jewish child.

This was later in our stay in Umbria, after our little night of violence, after everything was calm.

It was occasioned by a letter from Oksana indicating she might be coming to stay with us for one night or two. She had left Herbert. Her destination was unclear. Holly knew from previous conversations that Oksana hadn't wanted to have a child. So Oksana was in the air, or children were in the air. My son was twenty. I had perhaps not been a great father, but was at least trying now. We were under the trellis outside the kitchen door watching the onset of evening, the low distant hills taking on their animal shapes. She had made us a pot of tea. It was not the first time I had noticed that Holly made a pot of tea when she had something on her mind. What I remember saying, about Oksana, was that she would make a rotten mother and she knew it. Holly disputed this. She would brook no criticism of her friend. I stuck to my opinion. I claimed more longstanding knowledge. "Would I?" she finally asked.

"Would you what?" I asked.

"In your humble opinion. Make a rotten mother."

"There's no way this comes out right."

"Of course there isn't. If you say yes, I'll hate you. If you say no, I'll tell you I want a baby."

"Is that what's going to happen?"

"Take your chances," she said.

So I did. I told her I had heard on the radio that it was supposed to rain tomorrow.

"Come on, Nils."

"Holly, you would make the most wonderful mother in the world," I said, "but I've just raised a child and I'm a little late in learning how to do it."

"Can't we talk about this? No. That sounds stupid and pushy. *Should* we talk about this? Am I crazy?"

"We are talking about it," I said.

"Just wanted to know your feelings. Just in general. In the most general way. I saw you playing with those kids today, in the village."

"They're nice kids," I said.

"Gordon? My old boyfriend? He wanted children. That was one of the things. And I remember feeling afterwards, the old biological clock's running, why don't I have his urgency?"

"They're not for everybody, you know."

"I know… But now…should I say this? Just tell me to shut up, I'll shut up. But every once in a while I wonder."

"Like now."

"Like now, I guess"

"It's been a sweet time here," I said.

"It has. And I probably just spoiled a perfectly good evening," she said.

"Actually, I think your reticence is charming."

"Do you?"

She leaned over and nuzzled me. I rubbed her neck.

Then I said what I said about a Jewish child and my native land. She pulled away, threw her head back, as though to get a better view.

"What do you mean?"

"Only that. Would you really want to bring another Jewish child into the world to grow up in Germany? Would you want to give Germany another chance with a Jewish child?"

She gripped her tea cup, sipped tea that had to be cold, nervously poured herself more. "I don't know what you're even talking about Germany for, this was a general discussion, there's lots of countries…"

"But I'm German, I work in Germany."

"I mean, you've worked in New York. You *have* worked in New York. But it's okay…I was only asking, only wondering…" Her voice hardened a little, struggling to regain confidence, to seem a little brave: "But to answer your question, about Germany. I don't know."

"It's one of the few things I do know about. It seems cruel," I said.

I thought then that I was meeting her honesty with mine, and it is possible I was. But whether I was or not, it was the beginning of the end of our vacation. We had been like two lovers playing chess late into the evening, and now the game was over. The next morning we received word about Oksana's crash.

HOLLY ANHOLT

Vacation

NILS'S ANCIENT, half-collapsing stone farmhouse sat in a short and narrow valley, little more than a *cul de sac*, forty minutes from Arezzo. It was a place he'd bought with four other people from his paper fifteen years before and it had no heat but a wood-burning stove. Sheep grazed on the hillsides above the farm. One gravel road led out of the valley and around to the village, but there was also a track over the hills to the village, and it was this we walked each morning, often in the rain, to get our coffee and hang around in the sole, eerily quiet café. The tourists had yet to make their springtime descent. I was happy enough for a few days. So many questions put aside, questions like avenging furies, that could take up your whole life and leave your carcass for mere birds. Look, here was life, too. Life without questions but with a village you could walk to, and a café you could linger in, and sheep and goats on the hill and olive and fig trees, and our neighbor for gossip, and the only shower in the house coming from a black hose that sat out in the yard like a fat cat heating up in the afternoon sun. For four days we walked, read books, spoke quietly about the migrating patterns of the geese, about tomatoes, about the Bay Bridge in San Francisco which Nils with unbelievable stubbornness refused to believe was longer than the Golden Gate

Bridge; about anything but the city we'd driven from. Then he asked me to beat him, which I did.

It was at first as if someone had called me by the wrong name. I knew it was me who'd been called but it still seemed like they had the wrong person. Aside from a little tussle with a Polish camp guard, violence was something I knew about only at cinematic distances. And yet Nils kept saying it was my anger he was aiming to draw out. It wasn't for him, it was for me. I'd told him he'd seemed aloof. And this was his answer. I saw no reason to oppose him in this. I saw no reason to say no. He'd even inverted the terms of the discussion. He told me he didn't want to instrumentalize me. I imagined that must be a term in German, that he was translating from the German, he whose English was usually as easy and idiomatic as mine. But I understood well enough. He was permitting *me* to instrumentalize *him*. That's what he really meant.

He looked so tortured. If you took a Christ by El Greco and laid him down flat, that's what he might have looked like. I couldn't imagine hurting him more than he was already hurt. But I did. But I didn't. The dialectics of such things, in which you could get so easily lost, and forget the bodies that for a few moments were ours.

I had no idea even what my hands would feel like. It's how little I knew. And for a little while it felt like nothing at all, nothing more than kneading or slapping dough, except I felt a little sad, and like a child, just the opposite of when I'd make dough with my mother, we'd bake cookies and I'd feel so grown up. He let his flesh go slack. It seemed scarcely alive, until my nails penetrated his skin and I saw his blood. Then he goaded me about my anger, find your anger, Holly, where's your anger, you must be angry, words like that, I felt he was hitting me harder with his words than I was hitting him with my hands, and when I saw the blood and heard those words, that's when I hit him harder. I was angry at him for goading me. I was angry with him for having blood. I made fists and my knuckles hurt just like in a cartoon and I had no idea anymore if I was hurting him or not.

Of course it had to do with sex. In the end it had to do with sex. I gave up more of myself that night than I ever had. And I was happy to have it gone. See my new naked self. See my soul burned in anger. It makes this high clear flame, and we throw our aloofness into it and out comes, as if it were alchemy, tenderness. Between two people who are close there is no such thing, I think, as a secret whole and entire, there will always be hints, half-revelations, alternative ways of transmitting the essential thing. One sleeps differently. One exhales, and inhales, the perfume of the secret. And then it's possible to be overwhelmed by the scent.

If I could name the names of my anger, it would surely be banal. I am embarrassed even now to try and say, I'll want to insert question marks so you'll know I don't quite believe. Hadn't I always had a blank spot where my sister had been, where my parents had been, where I had never been? And this boyfriend of mine, who was it asked him along, with his opinions, and his know-it-all, and care? We Jews, we don't need this shit. Just show us the money and leave us alone. You Germans with your stupid camps and your memory, who needed you, too? I could have lived without any of it, yet I couldn't.

So much flew away for a little while when I bent over Nils and found in him the cause of all my pain. What a joke, what a lie, maybe. But I will tell you one secret thing: Nils was found out too.

The following days were aftermath to our afternoon of violence. We didn't repeat what happened then; we didn't even mention it. On the contrary, the next time we made love it was tender and quiet. Yet our little world was changed. Nils seemed more relaxed, more energetic, easier, lazier. I caught him playing with some village kids in front of the café. And I seemed to love him more. His life, my life, even the crazy, proverbial stretch provisionally titled our life, made a little more sense. The gulf between inside and out, that ordinarily seemed so immense that only the occasional lucky stab of imagination or circumstance could bridge it, lost some of its substantiality. If it was a void, if it was a mirage, could I not live more directly? I began to hate the circuitous, underground patterns of my life, the rooting-around in a maze, the guilt-ridden going ten blocks around to get one block from where I started. Anger. Anger was my magic bullet. I sang its praises in my heart. Fire was destructive until it was tamed. I would build a hearth and not let it get away.

A conversation we had once, in the evening, right out on the street by his apartment, before we left Berlin, on a night when the skinheads had attacked some African asylum-seekers and Nils had been out to cover the story, and he'd come back shaken, and I was shaken too:

"Nils…you know what's weird about being in Germany?… Or maybe it's just what I'm doing here, this property…or going out with you…I can never entirely shake this tin can that must be tied to me somewhere, this low level clanking away. 'Jewish.' 'Jew-ess.'"

"Is that so terrible?" he asked with an offhanded laugh.

"I don't relish the thinking about it all that much, frankly speaking."

"You'd rather be 'citizen of the world'."

"Of course," I said, and could feel the shape of my smile in my mouth.

Nils stopped on the sidewalk, quite dramatically, which wasn't his style at all. "You know something? It pisses me off, too! It pisses me off!"

"Hmm?"

His face was taut, his jaw drawn down. "Just like you, having to breathe the same stale shit all the time. Germans, fucking Germans, thinking about Germans, having to ask myself for the thousand and ninety-ninth times, what's going on with these people this time?"

His tirade was loud enough that I half-waited for windows to open, or buckets of water to be dropped on top of us, for anguished shouts to come tumbling down, like in a cartoon, "We're trying to get some goddamn sleep around here!" But no windows opened. Grosse Hamburger Strasse was still put to bed. A thought wrestled to escape my throat. It hardly seemed appropriate. "We…you…couldn't get away for a few days, could you?"

"Why in hell not?"

"I don't know, I mean, your work…"

"No, no, I'd love to," he grumbled. "We ought to. Go south."

And so that's how it was we came to Italy. Nils said to me once, and I believed him, I thought it was brilliant, that national destinies were way oversubscribed as determinants of personal fate, that they were mechanical and penny-ante, that if you wanted to find out how your life was shaped by larger things, in a way that at least poetry condoned, you ought to look to the stars the way they used to. Astrology trumped nationality any old day.

Of course this was from the same man who brought us the theory that the truest metaphor of love was Cupid's arrow. Or not even a metaphor, but a reality. Nils, who usually inhabited the sphere between ironic and laconic, could wind on about that one too. "Like the idea of a Muse, it speaks to the unlikelihood and lack of human control over something. People who say it's kitsch say so out of fear. They wish to make themselves 'open', they exaggerate their own will. They will tell you of course that love is a fairy tale, something from an earlier stage of human development, but even if they're right, they feel it is somehow possible, for them, love is possible, if they somehow make themselves deserving. No. Bullshit. When you keep an eye out for it, that's when you get in trouble. Better to be clear-eyed, better to go about one's business; and if Cupid strikes, then everyone will rush to say something about the person's character who was struck, they'll find aspects, they'll build a case, they'll add more crap to the lore and evidence about love. But they'll miss the point. Cupid will strike again, in ways unimaginable, and then the paradigm will change again."

Am I prejudicing the case against my boyfriend? I hope not. He had a wish to fix the world, I think. I recall his smile, his fretful look, his feelings of outrage, as if the world itself were an outrage. He was hard on himself.

Perhaps I was too. When we were in Italy, I received a letter from Oksana, saying she had left Herbert and was coming our way. I told Nils that much. What I didn't show him, until after her death, was this part of the letter:

"Franz came by," Oksana wrote. "He's leaving. Herbert gave him money. I eavesdropped, very blatantly, I'm afraid. Resigning from the Fund, from all of it. Time for a shack by the sea.

It's too comical, Herbert tells him, he says he can't suffer this many losses in a day (referring also to my leaving).

"Herbert said to Franz," she continued, "he only wished to know if he, Herbert, would be left holding some bag or other. Franz says his conscience is clear and that Rosen – do you know Franz calls himself sometimes by his last name? – is the bagman. Franz says, isn't that how it should be? Hasn't that been Rosen's job?"

Nor did I tell Nils that Oksana had taken files that might have implicated Franz. I didn't like it that Nils was going after him. Somehow I took it as a personal affront. Yet it weighed on me to have a secret from him, even when it wasn't much of a secret, that Franz was headed for a shack by the sea with a few marks from Herbert and a clear conscience. Give the fox a head start. Why not? But the hound was my own.

I know what Nils thinks, or once thought, but our conversation about children had nothing to do with us later breaking apart. It was a childish conversation. I regretted it immediately. Then there was Oksana's death and we had no more time.

HERBERT KAMINSKI

Accident

I'VE LIVED LONG ENOUGH that I try not to impute myth to fact. A car crash is a car crash. Accidents happen. Now I will record the facts as I know them: it happened near Puglia, on a hill road with many bends, a dangerous road, according to the Italian highway police. It was a road that had seen other accidents, other shrines. There was a second automobile involved, driven by a priest. The priest had a clean driving record and was familiar with the road. As he rounded the bend that was the site of the accident, the priest observed her car, with its headlights on, approaching at an uncertain speed while approximately one-half on the wrong side of the road. The priest took evasive actions, braking and swerving. She likewise swerved, but possibly did not brake immediately. She lost control of her car and it tumbled off the road into a ravine, rolling over twice or three times. Her car's airbag was deployed but was useless in this case. Her chest was impaled and her neck broken. The priest's car did not leave the road and he was uninjured. Her posthumous body was tested for the presence of alcohol and none was found. The same test was performed on the priest, with the same result. Further, her car was examined to determine if perhaps some mechanical failure, of the steering or braking systems, or a stuck accelerator, might have caused the accident. No such fault was found. When her body was returned to Berlin, I had the chance to observe it. Despite her injuries, her face in particular did not look injured. She looked like a baby bird that had fallen from its nest.

Now there were conditions precedent to this accident, certain situations. Before she left for Italy, we had a terrible quarrel. It was perhaps worse than this. I believed that she had left me for good. I could say that the "ordinary things" were said, the things that are always said in such quarrels, but I would be only saying this from what I've read in books. No one had ever said such things to me before. I had not had a wife, nor truly a lover, before. If they were not so hurtful, I would have found certain of the things she said banal. But again, this would have been only from having read them. "I am finished, I am trapped, my life is over," she said. Like a man fending off blows, putting up his hands, I said, "This is because you have nothing in your life." I was here referring to the fact that she had stopped painting, but she may not have understood. She often said that she detested shouting, yet she shouted at me, "Yes, yes, where you are, that's where there is nothing." Then she added: "If I stay with you, Herbert, everything you hoped from me will be gone. I can only hurt you now." Then she added to that: "This is the same thing I said to my first husband. I cannot ignore this fact. My life goes around and around."

The other situation was that she had recently despaired of her painting, which I've just mentioned. She had been working on a series inspired by the mosaics of the "brave Soviet airmen" in the Moscow subway, who appeared in her paintings like snowflakes barely crystallized over particles of dust, falling out of a clear sky. I found these, as I found nearly all her work, mystical and beautiful. I am aware that these are categories, particularly the beautiful, that many artists find pejorative and antique, but from my own view she should properly have gloried in them, and defied the right thinkers. I did not often surprise her at her studio, in the interests of not encroaching on her freedom. But on the afternoon before she left, I did, for reasons that seemed little more than chance. The studio had been constructed from a carriage house two kilometers' distance from our residence on Schwanenwerder Island. The side door was ajar. I knocked, of course, but my nose had caught a draft of sweet-smelling smoke. I walked in to find her stoking an oversized, nearly out-of-control fire in the fireplace with canvasses she had cut out of their frames. "What are you doing?" I cried. She was in one of her enormous white shirts and her face was smudged with the sweet-smelling smoke. What I recall now is her utter calm. "If you never do something like this, you can never start over," she said, almost as if proud. I moved towards the fire until its heat pressed me back. "They're beautiful, please don't, I'll take them and store them and never show them to you," I said.

"I'd rather they burn. If they exist, they're like children, I'll think about them," she said.

Then she held both her hands out towards me, and we embraced. We actually hugged each other. I held her fragile, small frame. But her voice remained high, defiant and clear. "There are very specific things in these I detest. Grandiose feelings. Even Franz noticed, he pointed them out to me. And about such things, he's invariably correct."

I studied my wife for clues, for signs of relenting, in what I saw clearly as a war she was waging against herself. That is, I saw it clearly until I did not. I began to think, who was I to say that's what it was? It was not simply that I felt tongue-tied with her. It's that I believed her intelligence was deeper and clearer than mine, that she saw things which I would be lucky to see later.

She took a few steps away from me, picked another rolled canvas off the floor, and without a further look threw it on the fire. It resisted the flames a few moments, then along its cylindrical length a brown curl formed and spread.

"You're making me terribly sad," I said.

"Then leave," she said, "I don't want to become sad myself."

I waited a moment, then backed away. "Don't be alarmed, Herbert," she said, and gave a careless wave to her work. "About these, I'm quite desperate. About my life, less so."

I nodded the sort of tight, aborted nod, little more than a seeming tic, that must inevitably suggest acquiescence more than conviction. Then I left. Outside, my eyes continued to water from the smoke. I sat in my car with tearing eyes and reddened throat telling myself that, after all, my wife might be right, or at least that there was no judging such things.

It might seem, from my arrangement of facts, that I am assembling a brief to propose a suicide, or a perhaps half-intended suicide. But this is not the case. I would only not wish to be accused of avoiding such evidence as exists. She either wished to live or she did not. It must also be said that she was a rather careless, inattentive driver, better than she had been, but still inattentive. And one thing more: when she left for Italy, it was with certain of my firm's financial records. Some cabinets had been ransacked. Our friend and my first assistant had recently resigned and gone missing, the result of a potential scandal hanging over him. I believe she had taken the files for him and was going to him.

A cremation was conducted in Berlin. There was no one

in Moscow who wished to claim her body back, and I would have opposed it in any event. Her mother now lives in Finland. We notified her, but she did not appear at the memorial. Of course there was no way to notify the father, if he is even alive, which no one believes. She died with a few friends, no family. In the pews was her first husband from Moscow. I recognized him from photographs, a slight, dark-eyed, dark-haired man, a poetic type, handsome, still young, altogether different from myself. I noticed him three or four times. He made the certain impression on me that he still loved her. A Russian choir sang at the service.

I consider that she led a lonely life. Like myself, she may have tried to believe that her loneliness was only prologue, that something in her life was supposed to happen next, in which loneliness would be redeemed, the holding out of her soul proving to be nothing more than that, a waiting game, time spent in the heart's antechamber. But we run out of chances.

Oksana. I write her name with difficulty. Oksana.

HOLLY ANHOLT

Education

A SAMPLER of what I learned from Oksana.

That the biggest casualties of the Wall coming down were the love affairs, since the Wall had been the shield for Western husbands. As soon as the Wall fell, the East German girls came looking for their boyfriends. Utter terror was spread. I heard Oksana express this considered judgment, very definitively, to a French reporter eager to question her about East-West relations, at her wedding party, of all places. Oksana projected an air of unspeakable melancholy. She was frail, yet when she spoke, in a lilting soprano, it was often in terms so definite it seemed as if she were fighting back against something, mounting some veiled yet definitive rebuttal, or launching a surprise counterattack. Even when the "something" wasn't apparent, as though the "something" must be confined in the precincts of her mind. And she wanted no part in politics at all. Everything was a stage for the personal. Politics had been enough in her life, and had only injured her. In this sense, perhaps, Simona Jastrow was no more than her distorted mirror image.

That in the Soviet Union everyone had bad teeth because there was no decent dentistry, and there weren't any bananas which was as good a proof as any that it was not a normal country.

That the reason David was Nils' friend was the German soft spot for oracular, posturing buffoons. She offered this in my defense at a moment when I'd only just met him and he was harassing me. But by the time I absorbed the lesson, she had grown rather fond of him, as someone who excited the antennae of her antipathy, which was better than no excitement at all. And I felt challenged to follow her suit, as I had a number of times with Oksana, the force of her frail, persevering personality working its way through me in an underground channel. I remember in particular a day the four of us rowed on the Wannsee. A December afternoon had turned unseasonably warm. We set out from the dock on Herbert's property. Nils rowed in clean, strong strokes, Oksana trailed her fingers in the chilly water, and David sat next to her with his shoes and socks in his lap, a roly-poly city boy in the country, making a joke or two about how he alone might tip the boat but otherwise oddly subdued that afternoon, as if there were no one there to impress. And I remember thinking: Oksana has tamed him. We were like two old couples that afternoon. Though I don't imagine she ever slept with him. For Oksana, sex functioned as some sort of junior lieutenant to her curiosity, something which I didn't so much learn from her as yearn to understand. But I don't think she was so curious about David. She seemed to know him too well already.

That it doesn't take long to make a friend. She invited me to her wedding party on the first night we met at Anja's. She must have identified me as part of her guild of exiles.

That the once-notorious spy Mischa Lander was another one who had a foolish crush on her, but his crush didn't stop him from trying to shake her down. I was virtually there when it happened, one of those moments as cliché-ridden concerning Berlin as, say, seeing movie stars in restaurants in Los Angeles. On a rainy day in early March, I visited Oksana in her studio. The phone rang repeatedly until at last she picked it up, seeming to know who it would be. Her side of the conversation that followed was punctuated by resentments and objections. "My car is in the repair… I'm bored with your threats… What files? What files?… I don't even know where he keeps such things… I assure you I will not… Well tell them then. Go to Axel Springer for all I care!"

I overheard all this, first with studied detachment, then with a rooting interest for my friend, and finally with fear. She hung up on him and went back to her dabbling brush, but within seconds threw it down. "I suppose I should see what he wants. Absorb his latest threats, I imagine will be more like it." So I drove her over. We were always driving each other places. Something else I learned from Oksana, that a good way to develop a friendship is to be always driving with the other one somewhere. She would call me up and ask me to drive with her to this place or that, most often only because she didn't wish to be alone. It was in this spirit, too, that I took her to meet Mischa Lander in a Grunewald laundromat where he was washing his clothes. On the way she was not embarrassed to tell me more. Lander had been well-connected in Moscow, she had once solicited him for help in locating her disappeared father (a solicitation which resulted in a brief affair), and he knew a lot about her past, which had had its inglorious aspects. She had been a translator for visiting businessmen, and a hostess as well, of very high morals, she said, which meant she didn't sleep with her Western clients, she only arranged for them to sleep with KGB women who photographed their sleeping nakedness and rifled their attachés. It was how she met Herbert. Who in Lander's estimation would not wish this bit, embarrassingly framed, to be known by *Stern*.

Oksana had no ulterior motive in telling me any of this, it wasn't as if she expected me to pass it on to Nils or hold onto it just in case, nor did it seem she was telling me secrets the way people often tell secrets, to prove to themselves that they're unafraid. She simply told me her life as a friend. And perhaps with, somewhere in there, the defiance of the fatally bored: what were they going to do, take her out and shoot her? She found all of it preposterous and trivial. But she had never quite put Herbert in the loop. Now Lander wanted, for sure, something to persuade Herbert to help him get out of Germany. "But he'll get nothing from me, I assure you. Not even a smile," she said.

I followed Oksana's instructions to a commercial street in Grunewald. The light of day, such as it was, was gone. We stopped across the street from the fluorescent-bright laundromat. Through rain-streaked windows we could see Lander inside, in a dark coat and tie like some newly arrived ambassador-without-credentials from a tin-pot regime that had been overthrown, removing his clothes from a dryer and dumping them on a table. No one else was in the laundromat. The scene had the dreary clarity of an Ashcan School painting. Lander held up a pair of socks that must have shrunk. He scowled, attempted to stretch them. He scowled again. He stretched again. Oksana said, "Don't wait for me." "But how will you get home?" I asked. She answered with a little wave and got out of the car, jumping across puddles to the curb.

So I drove away. It was the last time I saw her, except for her body in the back of the mortuary van on the road where she died. Nils and I, choric figures with too few lines, identified her.

That she would forgive me if I once confused who she was. It happened later, as Nils and I argued, back in his farmhouse, over why Oksana had run away with Herbert's files. "She was in love with you," I said out of the blue.

"What?"

"She was in love with you and she stole those records for you. She was bringing them to you," I said.

"I have an opposite, more realistic interpretation," he said. "She was highly indifferent to me, and she stole them for her own protection."

"Helena wasn't like that," I said.

"Helena?"

"Did I say 'Helena'? Oksana."

My friend, did you hear that?

FRANZ ROSEN

Painting

I WROTE ELSEWHERE about my "greatest fear." Perhaps this was hyperbole. In all events, an addendum is in order.

I spoke with Oksana once about her paintings. The airmen, the limpid Russian sky, a summer day. A kind of realism which doesn't trust itself, which I feel is the only proper kind. She was one who appeared very definite about what she knew, yet her work was entirely about what she couldn't know. The explication of a world, perhaps akin to Turner's, where light is all. And light consumes. Explication of course has no value there. You are dooming yourself to a tragic defeat.

I said to her one day that there was a grandeur to her effort. As I later learned, she interpreted what I said to mean grandiosity. I've considered whether this was an error in comprehension or translation, but it seems unlikely. She was a keen student of language. She was alert to nuance. So I've come to ask myself: how is it, what was it about her, so keen, so precise and observant, that caused her, in effect, to twist my words into something so hurtful to herself and her efforts? Or more tellingly, about myself: how could I not have seen it coming? Not *it* precisely, perhaps, but some such defeat. Why was I not able to take greater care?

I remember being so admiring and I remember her nodding,

in a noncommittal fashion, and saying nothing, until the subject was passed, until we had turned away from the wall where those lovely pictures were hung. One cannot force words out of someone. One cannot child-proof the world. And of course Oksana was the farthest thing from a child.

But I might still have imagined what a thin wire she walked. I might have seen more clearly behind the bravura intellect. I might have guessed, from the paintings themselves, how the landscape of her mind was laced with unmapped crevasses.

To turn the world against oneself is not rare. To be helped along by others in this accomplishment is a commonplace. Like the others, I am an agnostic about the cause of her death. But still, I can imagine myself shaking her, or my words, anyway, shaking her, "Oksana, please, why do you say that, that's not what I said at all. It's not what I said at all."

FRANZ ROSEN

Hatred

I AM THINKING OF HERBERT now, and not Oksana directly. But I believe one certain trait of his allowed him to be her protector. He is not a good hater. Perhaps to compensate for this emotional shortcoming, he has an enlarged ability to deflect or in some cases absorb the arrows shot at him.

I suppose the same could be said of myself. It's even possible, though I've made no general survey to support the idea, that this vitamin deficiency, as it were, was an adaptive trait for those few of us who remained here after the war. A case of survival of the fittest. Those who hated could have been driven insane.

(I might further observe that this Darwinian case is made in exactly the opposite fashion by some concerning the Jews before the war – it is said that if we had hated more, we might have survived better. But times change.)

(Moreover some of these same critics conflate hatred with courage. It is said that we feared to hate. But Herbert is surely no coward, either in business or anything else. For the smallest proof of it: no coward would have taken on Oksana.)

NILS SCHREIBER

Story

I CAN SUMMARIZE THE "INTRIGUE" in a paragraph. One of the top Stasi men was of hitherto well-obscured Jewish origins. After the East German collapse, he became fearful of prosecution in the West. He wished to emigrate but no country would take him. Proving beyond doubt what rich veins of irony these old GDR autocrats were capable of opening, what mines of dark absurdist bitterness, this formerly conventional Communist anti-Zionist began a covert negotiation with Israel based on the Jewish law of return. The negotiation involved, as intermediaries, certain trustees of one of the Jewish reparation funds in Germany, and in particular, Franz Rosen and by extension his boss Herbert Kaminski. The Stasi man, Mischa Lander, brought what pressure he could on Rosen and Kaminksi to effect his purposes, and offered a large bribe as well: he could obtain from the collapsed GDR a million gas masks, which Israel was said to need. The Gulf War was approaching. Israel had good reason to fear gas attacks from Iraq. But even in such conditions, Israel refused to accept Lander's offer. It said it had enough gas masks anyway. What it did not say was that it felt it could not afford to alienate our newly powerful, reunited Germany. Franz Rosen, the trustee of the reparation fund and a wartime Berlin hero, was distressed by the collapse of this deal. For some time he had had a Palestinian lover, a young man who persuaded him that, yes, Israel had perhaps enough gas masks to protect its citizens, but few for all the Arabs in its occupied territories, who, given the erratic tendencies both of gas and Saddam's likely ballistics, were in as grave a danger as the Israelis. Whether this was accurate or not I cannot say, but Franz Rosen was both distressed and outraged by what he took to be a moral lapse on Israel's part. So he skimmed the interest from the reparation fund which he was managing and bought the gas masks himself, intending to deliver them to entities in the occupied territories for distribution there. I learned about the skimming from records which our friend Oksana had "borrowed" from her husband, and which were in the trunk of her car when she died in the crash. I had to bribe the Italian highway police to get hold of the suitcase which contained them. Most of the rest of the story I got from Franz's Palestinian boyfriend, who had been betraying him right along, revealing to me Franz's crime in order, presumably, to embarrass Israel in Germany at a delicate time. I came to believe, without actual proof, that this boyfriend was acting as an agent for one of the frontline Arab states, perhaps Syria. In all events, I "caught" Franz Rosen.

A long paragraph, but there it is. But the "intrigue" was not the real story, in my view. The real story, in my view, had to do with my newspaper, and journalistic standards, and ethics. I presented the story to my paper fairly much as I had put it together. My editor refused to publish. And why? For a complete answer you would have to know the financial straits that our *alternativ* paper found itself in that year. Like much of Berlin's cultural life, it had come into being through the help of grants. Throughout the Cold War, the Western powers had been eager to promote West Berlin as a cultural capital. Now that the Cold War was over, and the vast expenses of reunification were upon us, such grants began quickly to seem superfluous. Our paper, which had been fine and brave in its best days and plain silly in others, was in danger of going under.

This is what Kröller, my editor, said, in response to my story: "It's premature, Schreiber."

I had worked on the piece for months. I had five key facts down incontrovertibly. I flew into my version of a rage, which was to feel my voice get as tight as my neck. "Premature? You wait much longer, you wait till the war's over, you'll have to put the story in a walker."

"You haven't given Rosen chance to rebut."

"How can I? He's fled, he's gone to ground."

"Find him."

"Oh for God's sake. Do you wait to publish every crime story till the criminal's caught?"

"Besides…Herbert Kaminski has reimbursed the reparation fund."

"What?"

"Out of his own pocket. I was waiting for you to walk in here. Kaminski himself called. No harm done. Completely mortified about the entire incident."

"And doesn't want the story out."

"Now you can drop the sarcasm, alright? You, Schreiber, of all people, ought to be sensitive, in Germany you don't implicate a Jew in a financial scandal before you have all the facts straight."

So that was that. Or not quite that. Forty-eight hours later it was happily announced that the Herbert Kaminski Foundation had made a four million mark grant to our prize-winning *alternativ* paper so that it could continue its fearless brand of journalism. A "no strings attached" grant, a lifesaver, a tribute as well to the brokenhearted integrity of Herbert Kaminski, who put his deceased wife's name onto the gift as well. Kröller phoned me with the brilliant news. He liberally sprinkled the phrase "no strings attached." He promised me if I found Franz Rosen, he would reconsider publication.

And even this wasn't the whole story, if you bothered to ask my heart. The whole story my heart would nominate would have to include my number one girl, who in the months I'd known her, until his disappearance, had grown increasingly close to Franz Rosen. They kept bumping into each other and then Holly discovered that Rosen's uncle had had a summer house on the lake where her parents had theirs. They met in a piano bar to discuss this and Holly came home in tears. It was the first time I'd seen her in tears. She told me their conversation word for word. It had begun with Holly herself telling Franz that her parents had been happy at their summer house, that it was why she was pursuing her claim, that it was the happy time of their lives. To which, *per* my number one girl, Franz replied: "Yes, perhaps they were. Of course within the limits of each person's capacity for such things. My uncle certainly felt arrived, pleased with himself. This self-, I don't know what to call it, self-something, self-acceptance, I suppose, despite all the bad conscience of the Jew in Germany. Being told you're rootless. Being told you didn't belong. In all sorts of books and so on. And then looking at the land beneath your feet and it's all true… You've trod it for however many years, but never enough, and a little slip of paper obtained through other little slips of paper says it's yours. And blood, and most of seventy million people, saying, not really, you never bled for this land… Such a barbaric concept, don't you agree? To have to bleed for land for it to be yours. Though even this game we played! The lists drawn up, the accountings, of the Jews that fought and died in 1914… Of course, I speak out of my feelings, perhaps not your father's or mother's whatsoever."

Or perhaps I've filled in a few of his words. But a few such words can make a friend forever. Thereafter Holly was his defender whenever the subject of Franz came up, which it inevitably did, since I was working on it all the time. Once she told me that I was only doing it for the irony of it all. Another time she asked me if I was enjoying my little ironic turns over her body.

"Your body?" I asked incredulously.

"It's how it feels, yes. You slay Franz, you slay me."

"That's unfair."

"At least it's not ironic," she said.

HOLLY ANHOLT

Franz

HIS INDISPENSIBLE QUALITY WAS his grace. You never saw him in a rush. He never moved in a rush. His opinions were considered and he spoke with the sort of calm I associate with works of art – particularly Japanese works – that seem to view the world from some point beyond it, that seem capable of stepping outside and looking back. I suppose he was backward-looking. Things didn't surprise him. In this, he was a good match for Nils.

Then there was that topcoat of his, or overcoat, whatever is called that long dark coat in wool or gabardine. Or there must have been more than one of them. Like an undertaker, he would wear it even in mild weather. He must have felt ill-at-ease without that protection.

He had a large head and I would say that he had happy eyes, they could seem to swim in that large head like tiny, sparkling fish.

I suppose he had a gay man's little belly, and rosy cheeks, so that he could seem elfin, even if he was over six feet tall. His hands were enormous and a little bit thick, like the paws of a puppy you could expect to grow huge.

What else? Anything else? I loved his voice, which was unusually steady, through thick and thin, and which I think you would call a baritone. It was a voice that made me want to listen and fall sweetly asleep at the same time. Or maybe it was the voice that made me sleepy and the words that kept me awake. The uncle I never had.

FRANZ ROSEN

Exile

WHAT IS IT ABOUT MY NATIVE CITY? Because of the wars, it is mostly too new. What is old in it is often elephantine and suffocating. It has no charming medieval town. It is replete with bad smells, gasses that come from who knows where, as though it suffered from gastric distress. The light is pale and weak. The cruelty of its history speaks for itself. It harbors more than its share of rough characters. Its sense of time is disjointed and extreme. Everything there becomes tiresomely political. The inhabitants cannot be said to be well-dressed or elegant or beautiful, at least not to a notable degree. The food is what it is. The distances to get from here to there are enormous.

These are my complaints. Yet I flee to Sicily where it is very pleasant and long every day to return. It is where the subway lines move as my mind moves, where the streets are mostly where they were when I had my joy in them.

NILS SCHREIBER

Rejection

THE NIGHT THAT KRÖLLER turned down my story for being "premature," there was hardly a thing in the apartment I managed not to stumble into. At last Holly had had enough of my childishness and I was forced to tell her. My certainty that Kröller was in the wrong perhaps failed to convince her, likewise my threats to take the story to another paper.

"You'd be gone then. You'd lose your job."

She seemed worried for me then. A pleasing thought, to have someone worried for you. But of course in my anger I had looked right past her. What she was really thinking was that she *should* feel badly for me, for my frustration and sense of futility and injustice, but that in reality she didn't quite. All the doubts she'd ever had about my pursuit of Franz came freshly into focus. She was unused to me being certain about anything, which was understandable, since I never was. It alarmed her. "But if it *is* early in the story…" she finally said.

And she said it a little sadly.

My mind wheeled around her. "With Herbert reimbursing, the thing's already deflating! Do you want me to wait till the other papers get it on their own?"

"No, but what *is* the story?"

"The story is, someone embezzles millions out of a public trust."

"What did he do with the money?"

"That comes out next. Either a trail of paper leads to the gas masks, or he's cached the money away and whatever he got from Herbert was simply a kiss goodbye. Are you going to make me feel guilty about this?"

"No. But… I do think…I'm trying to think…of the consequences, that's all. You publish, and a noble life gets smeared with shitty innuendo…"

"I didn't do it! He did it!"

"For decent reasons, maybe."

"The decent reasons will be there! I'm not out to crucify him! Listen, Holly, you haven't been here, you don't know. There's been a taboo in the German press for years about the Jewish community and money. Somebody stole millions from a reparations fund a few years ago, it disappeared off the news pages in days. Such coverage, as they say, is not kosher."

"But understandable?" I heard her question mark, so faint as to barely make an impression, a stamp made with only just enough ink.

"Of course, you mean our history, the desire not to revive slanders. But now it's time to take the next step. We have to afford to be honest. We have to afford to be normal."

Then she said the sort of thing which I knew embarrassed her to say, which surely she never thought she would hear herself say, and not only for its rhetorical flourish: "Maybe you think it's one more irony, Nils, the philo-Semite writing the story that services anti-Semite agendas. But for all the millions who only see the headlines…and for all the people who just want some shred of justification, some bit of excuse, for what happened to the Jews here…"

"I can't help them! They're sick! They're insane! I have to live for something better! We all do!"

Including Holly, I did not say, but of course she heard it anyway. Would she, after all, be an exception? What dose of self-pity or mortification gave her a free pass? Her boyfriend's a reporter. Reporters report. If everyone's lucky, they report the truth. When they do not, not when they do, is when the problems begin. Yes? No? Holly, please: yes or no?

She found herself shaking her head, a tablespoon in sorrow, a teaspoon in confusion. "I know. I know I'm wrong. But you're hard, Nils. You're really hard," she said.

She raised her eyes to mine. It seemed a long time that we searched each other. But such searches can leave false impressions; they can be nothing more than holding actions, when two people don't know what else to say or do.

Into this stalemate of the heart Holly spoke quietly. "Oksana said something once – I've never quite gotten it out of my head…probably because it was the only thing she said to me that I was sure was dead wrong…about you and her, you and Oksana…Two needy people, she said, shouldn't 'hook up'… she used that silly kids' phrase, those silly kids' phrases, like for once her ear was off… But you know her ear was never really off…Nils, I don't know…"

She came close to me and tipped her head into my chest. I held her, but a strange resistance, which felt to be neither mine nor hers, but perhaps only some random magnetic field that had slipped in to fill the air between us, stopped my arms from drawing her in. Finally she stepped back. "Something's off. It is, isn't it? It's gone…I don't know where it's gone."

"Is it the baby? Your wanting a baby?" I said.

"No. You were right to say what you said. At least you were

honest… And I was arrogant. Still am, I think, can't stop, keep thinking, acting, I don't know, like I'm this candle or something, this white candle, this moral candle. Nils, I know I'm not. In my best moments I know that… And I'm not your dark whore, either."

"And I suppose I'm not as billed, either," I said. "The good German, big-necked and rough-and-tumble, arriving just in time to save you and all of yours from the licking flames, repulse the butchering hoards from your door. I wish I could, really. But leaving aside the failings you've well-documented, the irony I'm terrified to abandon for more than a minute and all the rest – you're not in any fire, the hoards are taking a rest."

So we live with the shadows of others until we're confused, and then we live happily with the confusion awhile, and then it clears.

The room seemed very small, like a room in an old slum, with cracked paint and a sagging bed, where an amnesiac wakes up.

Several weeks then passed, and my number one girl became her own again, while I searched for Franz Rosen up and down the boot of Italy until I found him. A lot of bribes in seaside towns and then there he was, in a printed silk shirt and incongruous dark shoes, on a patio with a patio drink overlooking the sea. I told him I was ready to publish, though not that I had little idea whether Kröller would go along. I showed him what I had. He read with detached interest, nodding here and there, correcting a detail or two I'd acquired in the weeks or months of his flight. The gas masks were back in the eastern warehouse by now. A five percent profit had been made. The war was over. My story was certainly stale. For a little while I imagined that his graciousness was due to the fact that he knew he had outrun me; the victor's easy largesse. But it wasn't that. It was more, I think, that he'd found in me someone he imagined to trust with the secret which harried him more relentlessly than I ever had.

Or, simply, it was a gift he chose to make to me. I wrote everything he told me. "A Scarcely Possible Life." Kröller was pleased. He told me I'd written something at last that was more "human" than "political". Well, fuck him. Fuck Kröller. There was only one critic I was interested in hearing from.

It was two weeks before a letter came, postmarked Velden am Moritzsee. "Dear Nils, I'm well enough. The house may soon be mine! I suppose 'ours' is the correct pronoun. Anja did some digging and the claim on the country house is apparently near the top of the bureaucrats' pile. In the course of weeks that I've been coming out here, this thought has filled me alternately with dread and possibility. You used to call the two of us sociologists. But I believe I've become more an archaeologist, sifting through the ruins of the lives that bred me. I see I wrote, just a few sentences ago, 'The house may soon be mine!' But actually I doubt the exclamation mark is justified. I've moved out here full-time and am living with neurotics and paranoids in a dark, heavy house that as far as I can tell hasn't even a stick of my parents' furniture. Everything with the possible exception of the birdhouse is institutional, and GDR cheesy, even the refrigerator feels like it was made with the plastic they use in PEZ dispensers. And a guy across the road hung himself after setting fire to the claims office. This is some indication that I might not be popular here. Someone else left some old Nazi propaganda on my windshield. Am I becoming thick-skinned? I seem to wave these things off now. My goal, I've decided, is to discover where my parents hid in the woods. There is a bunker somewhere and one of the old Writers Union housekeepers has promised to find it for me. I am more aware than ever that there is some dark hole in my life that needs to be filled with light.

"But none of this is why I'm writing you. I'm writing on account of your piece. It's wonderful, from the very first words. 'Franz Rosen asked of me only that I tell the story of one queer Jew in Germany exactly as I saw it.' I've been going around quoting all kinds of lines from the piece in my head. I could imagine Franz standing there, his glass held high, with savage self-mockery, saying, 'You know when people are most easily made fools of, don't you? When they wish to be the hero.' What astonished me, really, was the sympathy. I've read dozens of your articles, but never one where you were so much a part of the picture. I could hear you in every choice, in every phrase, even when you were being only 'objective'. And that photograph of Franz, the perfect part in his hair, the thin starved face, the intense theatrical eyes. How old must he have been? Seventeen? And for what special occasion had he gone to the photographer's studio? You got that right, too. Finally I began to understand your point of reference, your argument, and saw that it was the same one you'd once applied to my father: everything Franz had done had been to overcome a humiliation imposed on him without his choice, yet it was a humiliation he was fundamentally powerless to undo. The best he could do was live with it, make choices accordingly, play the heroic fool, or the 'realist,' or whatever else.

"And then, Nils, I wondered: wasn't the same true of you?

"Who in that sense was far more a Jew than I was, so no wonder I couldn't live with you. Well that's a joke, I suppose, or half an insight in search of its whole. But I did imagine, just a little while ago, sitting with my coffee in the faux-leather armchair that was never my father's and reading your article a fifth time through, that I had begun to think like David, or like you. Nils the spirit Jew. Was it the murdered Jews' only revenge to turn the next generation of Germans, or at least its best and brightest, into themselves? Or did it work the other way? Did the Germans steal the Jews' lightning out of their corpses and pack it into their children?

"One could of course go on that way. Who cares, finally? But I admired you so much just then, as a reporter, as a lonely seer. I'm embarrassed, really, that I doubted you. But of course I had to."

And then her name.

HOLLY ANHOLT

Silence

WE HARDLY TALKED about what had happened between us. We didn't "rehash" or think to start again.

Was our silence the proof, as Nils might have thought, that our conspiracy of guilt had fallen apart? Or of what Oksana in her borrowed, birdlike English said, two needy people shouldn't hook up?

Maybe we were just stupidly brave and stoical.

And my anger, that magic bullet of mine? I could remember its name but not its feeling. I remembered it in sorrow.

HOLLY ANHOLT

Incidents

TO ELABORATE ON CERTAIN INCIDENTS which took place:

1. The first time I went into Simona's room, which had been my parents' bedroom, I was shocked by how bright it was, considering how dark and dreary was the rest of the place. Simona had painted the walls as white as any artist's loft. A jasmine bedspread covered the single bed. White linens lay on the dresser and bedside table. And meanwhile the sun had broken through, splashing a shaft of light through the curtained window. I went to the window. Pulling the curtain back, I stared out at the water. The sun that had broken through clouds in the west put a yellow late afternoon cast on everything it touched. The lake water was as calm as in a landscape of Corot. And for a moment, standing there, I thought I came closer to my mother. Young and strong. Her face unlined, in a cotton frock. *I will walk in the woods today. I will sit down by a brook. I will sit down by a brook with Helena on a blanket next to me and give her drinks of water from the brook.* I felt something of all of that. I felt my mother's confidence, my mother's hopefulness, my mother's easy grace with her baby.

2. When I first saw my neighbor across the street, he had a

broom in his hands and was shooing a woman off his stubbly front yard. The woman had arrived in a chocolate brown Mercedes with license plates of the West which she had parked in front of his shabby stuccoed house. She had expensive, piled-up hair and wore a designer ski parka with a variety of bells and whistles hanging off it. My neighbor himself was a ravaged-looking man with thinning hair and a mouth knit tight by repression, probably in his forties but who could know for sure. "Plant your own garden!" he was shouting. "Sweep your own walk! Clean your own dogshit!"

"There's no need for that, Mr. Anspach", the woman said, backing away from the probes of his broom. "I'm simply trying to bring a little beauty…"

"You're trying to bring yourself, that's all! Colonist! Scavenger!…Here! Here! You!"

He looked at me suddenly. He picked up a stringy brown piece of plant life, roots and a lifeless stem. "Is this dead? Be impartial! Judge!"

"Of course it's dead! You uprooted it!" the woman shouted back at him, then she too turned to me: "I plant things. This insane man destroys everything."

"Every week she arrives. Her ladyship in her Stuttgart pig-mobile! To *ti*dy up! *Burgher*ize! I've had it!" Again he polled me: "Dead or alive?"

I could understand well enough, but was afraid to put my limited German into the equation of his rage. I shrugged as if I wanted no part of any of it and went inside, while he continued to shout at the woman.

But I had unfortunately not escaped Mr. Anspach's interest. How could I have? I must have been the talk of the neighborhood. Later he brought me, as a housewarming gift, he said, a green cake in the shape of a dollar sign. What a clever man, Mr. Anspach. Like a fool I tried to explain to him that I was neither a speculator nor a colonist, and that my parents had been forced to live in a bunker in the woods. I was always telling people that, hoping that someone would know something about it. "Why don't you claim the bunker?" Mr. Anspach replied dryly.

Then it was Mr. Anspach who opened a "Museum of Colonization" in his house. He spray-painted a bed sheet and hung it from an upstairs window to announce what it was, and he would stand out front in a disheveled state yelling "Entrance Free!" at people who passed in cars. I went in once myself, to prove to myself I had nothing to be afraid of and that I was an objective observer of such things.

It was a house where the windows were never open. What a musty, sad smell it had. The combined living room-kitchen had been converted, according to a scrawl on the wall, into a "ROOM OF FIRE." News and photographs of the fire at the Potsdam claims office were taped to the walls. Another scrawl on the wall opposite proclaimed "OUR GLORIOUS VICTORY." This appeared to be headline for more clippings and statements, including Anspach's own, arguing the possibility or expressing the hope that the claims process would be set back by the fire. A small room adjoining the kitchen was bannered "EXAMPLE: POHL" and was devoted to the comings and goings of the woman who had claimed Anspach's house, the Berliner with the big car. I felt very lucky that he didn't have a third room for "EXAMPLE: ANHOLT".

Later the police came and questioned Mr. Ansbach about the Potsdam fire. Simona told me he was their prime suspect.

Later still Mr. Anspach hung himself. I write this with a worldly matter-of-factness but in truth I was horrified. It was a night for one of Simona's awful séances and I was cooped up in my room with the door shut. Mrs. Baum, the housekeeper, burst in: "Herr Anspach!" She thrust her hand to her throat. "Kaput!"

In his "Room of Fire," Anspach hung from a water pipe. His wife was hysterical. Neighbors hung back and gaped. After a moment seeing all these people looking at his body as though it were a piñata, I went to the sink and found a knife. The way I would later explain this to myself, my seeming composure was because I was so depressed about Nils that nothing else could bother me that much. I placed a chair under the dangling body, got up on it, and began to slice through the rope. "Please," I said to Mrs. Baum.

She came forward, as though prepared at least to break the body's fall. Someone else put a second chair under it. Mrs. Baum then held Anspach's legs, supporting him somewhat, so that the rope would be less stretched and easier to cut. I positioned myself so as to avoid looking at Anspach's face. His body exuded sweat and urine. As a way to shut out everything else, I focused on the strands of hemp, letting themselves go one by one in response to the insistent incursions of the blade. But my arm weakened, and the rope was still thick. Giessen the caretaker, another of the Writers Union retainers, at last got up with me, on the second chair, and took the knife from my hands. He was strong enough, the rope split apart, and the three of us lowered Anspach's corpse to the floor, where his widow threw herself on it, shook it and slapped Anspach's face. I was trembling by then, and still trembled half an hour later. The police would not be coming till morning. Other neighbors finally pitched in, to cover Anspach's body and close his eyes. I went home. The séance was continuing. I crept upstairs and tried to read and felt nauseous.

3. I was returning one day from a shopping expedition with Simona when I saw what I thought was a flyer on my parked car's windshield. If it had been anywhere else, I would have assumed a pizza promotion or a parking ticket. In fact, it was an envelope lettered formally, in capitals: ANHOLT.

I put my things down and opened it.

Inside the envelope was a photocopy of a three panel cartoon. In the first panel, titled "So it was…", a grotesque, thick-nosed landlord with black stubble was forcing a fair young Germanic couple out of their home. In the second, titled "So it might be…", the Jew/landlord stood aside with pleasure as gargantuan Bolshevik apes with nails in their boots trampled the same fair German family. In the third panel, titled "So It Must Be!", a large, brave, powerful and handsome German wearing a swastika armband turned back the Bolshevik beasts, who turned tail along with the terrified Jewish landlord.

"An old Nazi propaganda," Simona said blankly. I would have thought it was Anspach's doing, but Anspach had been dead ten days.

4. The way to Velden from the city is the S-Bahn to Wannsee, and from the Wannsee terminus to Velden a bus. I fell asleep on the train, my cheek on my balled-up coat that I had wedged between my seat and the metal window frame. I must have heard the conductor call Grunewald. Later I wasn't even sure I woke up. That would explain what happened next. It was a weirdly deep sleep, brought on seemingly by my lack of sleep the night before, up worried over one thing and another, the claims that were coming up, the Schiessls, all of that all over again. I seemed to open my eyes. We were stopped for some reason just short of the station, in the middle of a freight yard.

Many tracks, many trains, strings of box cars and cattle cars. And I thought I heard someone, in English, maybe Nils's voice, though I didn't know it at the time, say to another person, "You know, the deportations took place from Grunewald. The transports left from here." And as I heard the words, uttered between two people I could not see, a freight train moved past my window. And car by car, I could see hands thrust through the wooden slots of the cattle cars, and faces, high and low, pressed against them, crowds of people in each car as in a documentary film. They seemed to be crying for help, some of them, at least, I could see the mouths of women moving, and children. But I couldn't hear their voices. Then the train jerked forward, and the passing freight was gone, and I was truly awake, sitting in an S-Bahn car in Grunewald station.

5. I wrote Nils that I was able to ignore the Nazi propaganda that I found on my windshield. That was true, but only for awhile. I thought I'd trashed it, I certainly should have, but a few weeks later found it in my things. It was about as welcome as a reminder for a dental checkup, but I gave it a second glance. And then – as I might have told myself – merely as an intellectual exercise, just to see if I could do it, I tried to imagine that my father was that Jew/landlord, with the number 6 nose and black stubble and his stomach overhanging his belt in the same cartoon shape of his nose and thick lips pursed with lust; my father as he might have been portrayed. Then to round out this nice picture I imagined my mother, rouged and furred, angled and decayed, an expressionist's rage. I worked this mental picture up until I could have passed them on the street without recognizing them. Not really a healthy exercise, I think.

HOLLY ANHOLT

Fear

THERE WAS NEVER A MOMENT when I entirely got over the anxiety I felt for having made my bargain with the Schiessls. Nobody, not Anja, not even Nils, could quite convince me that it was not in some way a fraud. Anja did her best. She explained that my parents were precisely the sort of people that the claims law was intended to benefit, and that I was of course their rightful heir and there was no reason there could not be a mutual rescission of the subsequent sale my father made to Schiessl, in the interests of justice and so on. But it still felt like a fraud. A little bit, anyway. And if it was a little bit fraudulent, wasn't I? I began to have fears that someone in the house, Simona or Mrs. Baum, would discover the little irregularity and hire a lawyer and it would be in all the papers, headlines to be imagined, but something about an American woman making a deal with Nazis to force some honest Germans out. The propaganda I found on my windshield of course aggravated those feelings.

Even the piece of paper with my father's signature, the bill of sale, caused me to cringe when I thought of it. The two pieces of paper, really; the Schiessls' copy and mine. I wished they didn't exist anymore, I wished I didn't have to think about them. But of course the Schiessls wouldn't want that; the pieces of paper were what they had to hold me to my end of the bargain. But then what was my hold on them? We hadn't even committed our arrangement to paper, the lawyers had agreed it was better not to, it was all done on a handshake. There were nights when I imagined the Schiessls finally taking it all, taking my inheritance, and what was I going to do? Anja said I could sue and win for sure. But would I really file a suit against the Nazis in which our whole deal together would come out? Even Nils would be tempted to write that one up for his paper.

With the news that our claim would be coming up soon, my fears intensified. I was living in Velden now. Was I really ready to sell it? I tried to imagine Anja going to their lawyer Rosenthaler with a little request, "you see my client is involved in this little psychodrama, she needs a little time, can we sell the place in a year or two?" Even the thought of dealing again with Rosenthaler disturbed me. And it disturbed me that I had never met the Schiessls, that I had gone a little bit out of my way not to, or it was they who were avoiding me. It seemed craven of me not to know what they looked like, what they sounded like. I should go, I should seek them out. Maybe they'd be like Nils' parents, maybe that was the template I should be considering, rosy-cheeked people who made jokes and baked all day. But I didn't believe that. I continued to believe that I'd made a pact with the devil.

And I missed Nils, missed the chance to sort it all out with him, to be held and advised.

DAVID FÜRST

Work

ONE STRATAGEM I DEVISED for revving the motor of Skin Enterprises was to get on the American television program *60 Minutes*. If we couldn't sell cars in Germany, why not America? Or better still, a rebound, the Germans discover my product through its popularity in the States. I present myself as a post-Cold War hero, the evil empire is slain, but into its ruins comes the enterprising hero, making free market lemonade from the old Commie lemons. And better still, for American tastes, the Jew and the neo-Nazis. I recalled from my three years in New York the phrase: what could be bad? I introduced this idea to my satisfied customer the American girl Holly Anholt on the day that she and I and her then-boyfriend Nils and our then-alive friend Oksana Koslova picnicked on the Wannsee.

"Well why not? You might as well try," she said. I could tell from her furrowed brow that she was trying very hard not to tell me that my idea was about as likely as a great white shark leaping out of the lake and eating our lunch but leaving us alone.

"Do you know anyone at *60 Minutes*?" I asked hopefully.

"Of course not."

"Just my luck, I meet one American a year, they know no one at *60 Minutes*."

She needn't have added that America is quite a large country, *et cetera*. It was only then I felt my bitter disappointment.

I made calls to the *60 Minutes* offices in New York, I sent special delivery letters and faxes. I continued to wait for a response.

It is no small sadness when others don't see the human interest in your case.

Though in this regard I have a small item to brag about. I did a wholly gratuitous favor for the American girl. I had not a single ulterior motive which I could accuse myself of. It was after she and Nils had split and she was living in the country all the time. I had a friend in Dahlem who had come into possession of a Greek pot and wanted an opinion as to its authenticity and quality. I recalled that such work or something much like it was what Miss Anholt had been doing in Paris. I phoned her up. She was both surprised, and, if I may say so, ecstatic. I heard later that she thought it was a terrible pot. But she continued to be grateful. She sent me a bottle of champagne.

HOLLY ANHOLT

Pot

A FOURTH CENTURY GREEK KRATER arrived by messenger in Velden, courtesy of David Fürst. It was a joy for me just to see the crate. My life went on. My life had continuity. Work makes you free, that cruel old cliché again, exhibit A for the slipperiness of words. But work anchored, anyway. Even a little work anchored. It was, when I got the packing straps and bubble wrap off it, a disappointing pot. Three young men chasing a dog, but the faces of all three men were obliterated and the dog was little more than a stick figure. Still, I allowed myself what I always allowed myself with artifacts, a few moments in an otherness so profound it seemed to wake me from the world I came from.

GERTRUDE BAUM

Sister

I WILL TELL YOU EVERYTHING. Why should I not? I have nothing to be ashamed of. People think we should be ashamed, but this is only because they think nothing of us. We are here. We have been here.

Of course for a certain period there were certain things we didn't say. I kept my peace as others did. You can call this hiding if you wish. I don't know what you call it, nor do I care. We are old people. Our lives are done. It would be better if you just left us alone.

But I'm not stupid. I see this is not possible. I can see that there is money involved. She comes to the Writers House and she denies this, of course. She denies this has to do with money and owning things. No, she says, this is about her parents, finding out this and that. We don't believe in these stupid things you see on the television. The American discovering herself. Oh please. We are in enough pain already. This was our attitude.

If you wish to explore, go discover America. Or better, go to the moon. Go do your exploring on the moon. Don't come here and tell us you're exploring. Explore what? Oh, please. Do you think we are Indians?

This also was our attitude.

She was not the only one, of course. If she was the only one, perhaps we could accept. There was also the woman who wanted Anspach's house. In her S car and her ski parka with jewels that must have cost thousands, telling Anspach he must tidy up, sweep his walk, for it would all soon be hers. Why should it soon be hers? Because her father lost it, Anspach should lose it now? I had no love of Anspach, you understand. What a seedy man. But no wonder his mind went over the cliff. He set a fire, you know. He set a fire and then he goes and hangs himself. If the police had not come, I don't know if he would have hung himself. The claims office. It was this he set fire to. You could read it in the news. If the deeds were lost, he thought, then claims couldn't be made. But he was mistaken. There must be copies somewhere. The police came. He hung himself.

He was a seedy man, but he had ideas. Do you know he turned his house into a museum? Museum of Colonization. Come see his photos! The woman in her parka, his tormentor! Even one or two of the American girl, who was ours! Do you know what he did to the American girl? I should not put it quite that way, did "to" her. He gave her a cake which he baked himself. He brought it to her. Then she sees that it is green and shaped like her American money. The sign for it. Everyone was very sober then. We didn't laugh. To laugh out loud, it would be impolite.

So Anspach hung himself from the rafter like a side of beef. But he was not a side of beef. Nor was he always this way. The changes did this to him.

Have you a picture yet of our village? I am not a busybody. Any who say so are jealous liars. It soon became impossible even to have a job without the others being jealous. This too, you see, we laid at their feet. Before, we were poor but we had jobs and houses. Poor jobs, poor houses, who cared? We were all the same.

Then comes Miss Anholt, the American girl. Miss Anholt this, Miss Anholt that. Who could not think of her? And with her terrible German. Yes, she could speak German, she would try, always, of course. But it was terrible, a child would not speak it. We should all speak English to her? Of course not, thank you very much. A thousand times better she should not understand us! And why was she "Miss," why was she not married? She was pretty enough. I'm not saying to be *still* married, but not married ever? This was curious. She made no sense, in our eyes. Or it was too difficult to see. She had money as well. So why never a husband? She must have a terrible flaw.

You see, when people wish to hold something against someone, they can find many things.

She came, the very first thing, she took her tray to her room. Now there is a sign in the kitchen, big as you please, DO NOT REMOVE TRAYS FROM KITCHEN. So I say something. Of course she pretends to be apologetic. The next thing I know, the next morning, she has taken everything back down to the kitchen, her tray, her tea, all of it. So I said to her, again, "If you do that, what is there for me to do? It's my job. I am housekeeper." You can't win with these people.

I asked her very plain, very polite, if the Writers House becomes yours, are you going to let us all go? Not only myself, but for Mrs. Kirschner also, and Giessen, I asked. Of course. I wouldn't ask only for myself. And she says to me, "I do not know." She didn't know! If she didn't know, what was she doing here? I said this to her. She had no answer at all. Again she apologized. I spit on apologies. What do they get you? Can you buy bread with an apology? Her apologies were only an excuse.

Now you will say, with all this hatred of her, how did I become the one who would help her? But I didn't hate her. Yes, I did not like her. I did not like her coming here. But why should I hate such a silly girl?

Of course she was silly. What else could we think? We can scarcely deal with today and she comes only thinking of yesterday. And because she is thinking of yesterday, our todays become harder. Did she notice this?

Oh yes, she says, I'm so sorry for this, so sorry for that. Then go home, Miss, and thank you very much.

But, oh, this wonderful past of hers. This is the joke, of course. This is where you see.

How many times, she talks on the telephone, not to me of course, but on the telephone, to this person or that person, all this about how happy her parents were, how happy they were when they were here.

But if they were happy, why did they hide in the woods? I'm not stupid. I understand. The fascists. All I am saying is that she viewed time one way when there were other ways too.

And then of course she wasn't content. If she could be content, that would be one thing. Alright, here is the house where they were happy, so sit and stare at the trees or the bookcases or whatever is so contentment-making and be content. But no sooner is she sitting here, then she wishes to find where they had to hide. She wishes to find their *dis*-content. So that she can be discontent herself? You see it makes no sense. She brings her discontent with her. It is our misfortune.

Again, I am not stupid. I understand that she wants the *whole story*. But why? At whose expense?

So, yes, no one helped her. No one said, "I'll help you with this or that." Until I did.

Why should they? They could be kicked out. She could make who knew what more problems. Isn't it always the messenger who is punished?

But then why did I? Because I have a big heart, of course. I have always had a big heart. Even my mother said so. She said, "Your big heart and your big mouth, together they'll get you in trouble, Trudi." Of course they have.

But how could I help myself? When Anspach hung himself, everyone gathered in his house. This was before the police came or the ambulance. Such a mad house, with all of poor Anspach's displays, all his photos and all. No one dared touch him. No one cut him down. He hung there. It was very sorry. Until Miss Anholt came. You know you hear these things, Americans do this and do that, it's all very unbelievable and silly, but in fact in this case Miss Anholt saw poor Anspach hanging, and who knew what she felt or why, but she took a stool and climbed on it. It was all very unbelievable. Everyone watched her as if she was as mad as Anspach, but in this case she wasn't mad, I suppose she just couldn't stand watching him hang there or some such thing. With a kitchen knife that Giessen passed her, she sawed on the rope, and even I, I admit, and Giessen, held her stool so she wouldn't fall – I believe Giessen also finally sawed as well, which was surprising to say the least – and when Anspach's poor body slumped, it slumped on us and on her, too, but we did get it to the floor and laid him out there.

So you see. This is why. Only this. A simple reason. She acted once like a human being.

You can't imagine the impression this made. Though on the

others, I'm less sure. Why did she do this? How did she do this, or even think to do this? Why didn't she only stand in horror and wait for the police? I believe, actually, she didn't know better.

Or she could have been, in her own way, as desperate as we are.

Then of course all the rest took a part, tidying him and so on like that. Fear of the police was forgotten.

So I gave her credit. I liked her better not at all. But you see I am a person with a proper mind, as well as having a big heart. It has cost me all my life, as now you know, but I could not avoid seeing that if she cuts Anspach down from the rafters, she becomes one of us, you see. Not that this is any too good a thing. Believe me, I liked her no better.

Still, I determined that I must finally approach her with the information, which of course was known by others as well – not by the young but certainly by the old, by some, whose names I could list but why would you care – the information that she was foolish to be looking for this concrete place in the Velden woods, which were too small to hide in, but she should be looking in the Karlsheim woods instead. I told her this, about the Karlsheim woods. I even offered to take her and show her.

So I am a proper person, as well as big-hearted. No one can deny this. I will not shed my tears, you will not see me shed my tears, but this is beside the point.

I did not intend to tell her everything. I only intended to show her where the hiding place was. If that's what she was looking for, then if she found it, maybe she would leave.

On a Saturday we set off to Karlsheim, which for those unfamiliar with our territory I would say is quite close to Velden. It is an easy walk, but it is not on the lake. I brought my walking stick just in case. I like to be prepared for all occasions, so I brought also hats for Miss Anholt as well as myself, hard-boiled eggs and orange soda, and a shovel.

The woods are thick in Karlsheim. Even I could become lost. They are thicker than the Velden woods because they are not on the lake and are less tended. I led the way. Miss Anholt looked very doubtful, as if possibly this was one more joke being played on her and suddenly Giessen and all the rest would jump out of the woods yelling "Surprise!" or something equally stupid. But no one jumped out. To the contrary, I got very lost and we saw no one at all. Again Miss Anholt felt doubtful. But I have always had a good directional sense, even when lost, I make a wild guess and somehow it is the direction to go in. This is another one of my good traits, my ability to get out of a corner. And so I did. After an hour in which I will say that I sweated like a dreadful pig and to some degree likewise Miss Anholt and we consumed all the orange soda, I found what she was looking for, even if I felt it entirely foolish for her to be looking for it. This was the bunker, which was from the other war, the first war, before I was even born, the other war we lost. It was a stupid-looking thing, so overgrown and ridiculous, even an animal would not wish to live in such a thing. But of course sometimes we have no choices left. As for another example of this, if Miss Anholt kicked me out, I myself would have nowhere to go, having lived at the Writers House twenty-four years. This I would not say to her, of course. It would be humiliating. But I will admit it could have colored my thinking, in terms of opening my heart to her and helping her.

As it happened, certain flowers were growing in the clearing where I found it. These were buttercups, I believe. There were also many puddles. The thing itself was very overgrown, yet I recognized it, for there could be nothing else like it. It was not as if they built many such things. It perhaps had been for practice. Who knows?

I said, "Yes. Here," and pointed with my stick.

Miss Anholt, I would say, stared at the spot as if it was a carcass, as if she was still staring at poor hanging Anspach. Of course she acted unsure, like she didn't wish to believe me.

"Yes. The bunker. Where they were. Yes," I repeated.

I was making myself entirely clear, even to one who could speak only a Turkish child's German. So she did not wish to believe me – but what choice did she have?

I was not going to dig out this thing myself. That wasn't part of my plan. I sat on a rock, leaning forward on my stick, while Miss Anholt dug. For an hour it was as if I were the boss and she was the slave. This felt pleasant enough, I must say. Miss Anholt took off her jacket when the sun broke through. Finally I offered to substitute for her, but I had shown her enough of my weak leg and I was not mistaken that she would decline. Finally she threw the shovel down. She had achieved a pile of dirt and roots, nothing more.

"I cannot find anything," Miss Anholt said.

"But I know this is where they hid," I said.

"*How* do you know?" she said.

And now you see how my big heart got in the way again. She was so pathetic and my disgust for the entire situation was so intense that it became inevitable that I would feel a certain sympathy for her. How else could I escape? All these hidden facts were already on the tip of my tongue. How could they not be? When you have a secret, the first thing is you wish to tell it. It's like a cat scratching at a door. All the time, let me out, let me out, let me play. So, yes, I told her more. I am not ashamed. It was only fair.

I said to her, first, to prepare her, of course: "You must not blame me."

Of course she did not understand this. I had to make myself still clearer. "Not my fault," I said, pointing to myself and waving a finger.

"For what?" Miss Anholt finally asked.

"I know a few things more."

This she understood. But now she was getting impatient and perhaps she even sensed how all along she had been despised by us all, so that now she was despising me back. "Please, no games, Mrs. Baum," she said.

"I knew they hid here...because Ute told me," I said.

"Ute?" She repeated the name. And actually, I thought, it was like she had heard this name somewhere before, as if she were trying to remember where.

Now it may seem like I was teasing the girl, but I was not at all. No matter what you think, I am not like that. No, I was simply deciding, with each word, each answer, whether to put my neck further into a noose that I could not see. And then what the devil, I would think, maybe it was her neck, and not mine, that was going there. "She died many years ago," I said, speaking extra clearly, as you speak to a child.

"Who was Ute?" On her face there was still great confusion.

So I repeated the following twice, and with gestures, so that she should understand: "I hardly knew her. She was older. She was better friends with my sister Marie."

Now she was so put out that all she could do was speak in English, a flood of words from which I could only pick out, like bodies in a rushing river, the fewest things to grab on to, "Marie," "Ute," "shit." Of course "shit" was a word in English that I knew. I was driving her mad. Though for sure I knew this already, that she was mad. Finally I pitied her. What else could you do with a madwoman?

I pushed myself up on my stick so that I could reach her with a hand out. "Ute…the mother…of your sister Karen," I said.

Now of course the madwoman accused *me* of madness, with her eyes. "What do you say? My sister was Helena."

"Your half-sister. *Half*-sister…" I chopped at my arm, ridiculously, to show what is "half". "Karen," I repeated.

I was beginning to think our dear Miss Anholt was not only mad but dense. But it must have dawned on her. "Karen?… My father?" she asked.

I felt quite proud of myself for having gotten through to such a slow person. So I went on, in the spirit of generosity: "It's true. I can take you to her. I can take you to Karen." My fingers ticked along, to show I could take her.

"Karen? My sister? Alive?" Miss Anholt's voice rose to quite a high level.

"Yes of course. In Karlsheim," I said.

This was all the digging we did for one day. Later I felt very definitely that she resented that we had not told her before, but it was impossible for me to explain to her how I had been influenced to have a change of heart. I did tell her, however, I explained, about Petra. Petra is Karen's other sister, Ute's other daughter, who cares for Karen. This, however, I did not immediately explain, that Karen needed caring for. I wished Miss Anholt to see and decide for herself. I hoped she would learn something from this.

"But does she know? Do they know?" This is Miss Anholt again being I shouldn't say naïve exactly. I pretended not to understand her question, or how she said it. She had a grave look that told me how important she felt it was. Really, her brow all curled up. I don't believe such looks.

"Does who know what?" I asked back.

"That Karen's father is not Petra's father. I can't go over there, 'oh, hello, Karen, my sister,' if…"

I stopped her right there. "Petra is not naïve," I said. "This is one thing Petra has never been." And only because I wished not to keep looking at that grim expression of hers any longer, I added, "Petra's father was also a ghost."

And when even this seemed to puzzle her, I flapped my arms like wings, to show how quickly that one disappeared into the night. You see it was never a picture of one happy family at Ute's.

"But Karen?" Miss Anholt keeps asking.

"You'll see, you'll see," I said.

I didn't care to say more. I didn't care to give away too much. As I previously mentioned, I wished Miss Anholt to decide for herself.

I understood for sure this was all for show, anyway, this concern of hers about who knew what. She intended to meet her sister in any event.

Now of course Petra was not exactly shocked that Karen's miraculous "sister" wished to visit her, as Miss Anholt's presence among us had been well-known to people for months. It was bound to be a matter of time, that sort of thing, Petra thought. When I called her on the telephone, she told me how she even made plans for this day, how much she already troubled herself to prepare Karen for such a "disturbance."

Nonetheless she says we must not come to see Karen for two days or three. And why is that? Because Karen has sneezed two or three times! But you see this is just like Petra, always to make a fuss of something, to place little difficulties. She is not at peace unless she is making something a little more difficult. "Oh no, don't come now, come later, call first, we'll have to see about this." This is Petra. She has always been this way. Even her mother said this. Ute, what a pity, her life. First Petra, then Karen. Such a life. It makes you glad to have no children. And such a husband as Jürg Fenstermacher? God relieve me.

But at last the day comes when, oh my, yes, now, the two or three sneezes all are stopped, come today at fifteen hundred thirty hours, not fifteen, not sixteen, fifteen hundred thirty precisely. But of course I was familiar with this behavior. What could be done? Fortunately Miss Anholt is a prompt person. This much I can say for her.

In the car to visit Karen, Miss Anholt asks me, clear as day, in perfectly good German, by the way, so that then I began to think she must be hiding from us her abilities, in order to eavesdrop or some such thing, she asks, "Mrs. Baum, do you know who turned in my parents?"

Perhaps she had only been practicing this sentence, to make it perfect. I said to her, "Miss Anholt, I don't know who."

This happened to be a lie. Many years ago I heard this story. Many years ago, when I was young. And why should I forget such things? But I objected to Miss Anholt's question. She asked too much. She wished to make too much trouble.

I added, however, and this was true: "For sure it was not Ute. She felt bad for your father. She brought them food. Always… Also, your father gave Ute money for Karen."

This made Miss Anholt's eyes quite wide.

"Of course. Ute said so. He was honorable."

I felt I should say this, that her father was honorable, in order that she be somewhat relieved, but then I could not in good conscience avoid explaining to her, "You know, it was illegal, then. For a German and a Jew…" And I made such gestures as she would understand, unmistakably, my meaning.

"Yes, I know it was illegal," she said, in a very chilled way, so that I knew it was true what I had thought, that she despised me.

But when you are a person such as myself, with my sense of how things should be, you do not let the feelings of the other person deter you. I had seen Miss Anholt on the previous evenings, sitting in the common room at the television, playing over and again a tape she possessed of her mother and her father. What she was looking for, God only knows! It was a very old tape. Or I suppose a new tape of an old film. Whatever it was. But I saw Miss Anholt's tears. It was the first time I had seen such a thing, and I must say it surprised me. She didn't seem that type of lady.

Petra's house is in Karlsheim, and it is very small, even for a house in Karlsheim.

The very first thing she says, so that you'll know at once what a great favor she is doing you, is "Karen has a cold still."

Very nervously Miss Anholt asks, "Would she like to see me?"

Of course Petra doesn't answer this. Instead she says, "This way," and leads us to the back room.

It is another thing about Petra, that she never likes to answer someone's question directly. She feels it is doing them too big a favor.

I will admit that I watched Miss Anholt's face quite carefully to see how she would react. She understood at once her sister's mental condition. Karen was sitting in bed in her nightgown. She was watching an American police program. Of course a box of tissues lay on the bed, but I could not tell if she needed them or if Petra had put the box there so we would be sure to know how much we were imposing.

"Karen, this is who I told you about," Petra said.

"It's almost the end," Karen said, as she was watching the police program very intently.

"It's almost the end of her program," Petra repeated to Miss Anholt.

So we all stood around while this very stupid program went on. Karen became very excited by it, however. This disturbed me. Why should her small brain be so interested in the television? Also she began to shout things out. "There! He's getting him now!" Such things as that. Her smile was very broad, very embarrassing. Miss Anholt was in quite a panic, I would say, though of course she said nothing.

"We turn this off now," Petra at last says. Karen protests. Petra insists. "But he caught the man. Yes? Look."

What grief! It was unbelievable. "But then he talks with Deedee about everything," Karen says.

I of course had no idea who this Deedee was, though perhaps Miss Anholt did, coming from America.

Now I recall the conversation between these "sisters," if you'll believe, as best I can.

"You know who I am?" Miss Anholt asks.

"From America?"

"Yes. I'm another sister."

"Yes. With Petra."

"I'm Holly."

"I know."

"I'm very happy you are my sister, Karen. I'm very happy to have a sister. You're my only one."

"Petra's not your sister?"

"No. You're lucky. You have two sisters."

I recall this conversation so well because I remember thinking, they speak exactly the same, it's a perfect match, the retarded one and the American.

Then Karen becomes weepy. I am not surprised, she is a weepy child, always, but Miss Anholt becomes upset to see this and reaches out towards her. Petra stops this at once, of course. No displays in her presence, please.

Of course she does not say this. Instead she says, to Miss Anholt, with as little respect as you can imagine, "You're not helping. She only cries because she misses the ending of her program."

So up goes the sound again. The police are discussing things. Karen becomes happy again. And so this is how Miss Anholt's first visit with Karen came to an end.

On the way home, exactly as I feared, Miss Anholt proclaims that now she wishes Karen to come visit her at the Writers House. This proves exactly the point that I always make. You cannot do a good deed for someone. They always want more.

So it is all arranged. After much fuss about her cold and who knows what not, and again making the times precise and other difficulties, Petra drove Karen to our house.

Miss Anholt was well-prepared for this. In truth for days all she did was prepare. She even went so far to set the hammock between the trees by the lake. She bought cakes and wanted everything to be very nice. It was like she was the mother, even, or the grandmother. It was something I could understand, but also not understand. But I had no say. She didn't ask me. Miss Anholt of course lost her interest in me once I had introduced her to her sister.

I will say that when I saw Karen again, up on her feet and so on, I was almost surprised, I had almost forgotten, what a big girl she was. She was by inches taller than Miss Anholt. And why do I call her a girl when she was fifty years old, with all grey hair and the usual flab and such? Because she was, that's all.

Miss Anholt had sandwiches and cakes for her and lemonade and swung her in the hammock. This was all as planned, and I was quite impressed. Miss Anholt, I thought, must really love her sister. And she was quite a good organizer of such things. I had scarcely a role at all, although of course I washed all the dishes.

Even when they walked by the lake, Petra was always the chaperone. It seemed Petra didn't quite trust Miss Anholt, perhaps she feared at any second that Miss Anholt might run off with Karen. Though why this would have alarmed Petra, who always complained about Karen, I wouldn't know. At a certain time Miss Anholt proposed that they both take off their shoes and put their toes in the lake. Petra raised objections, of course, there was no towel, Karen would catch sick again, but then, as occasionally was possible with Petra, she relented. I was there at this point and observed something very interesting. Both Karen and Miss Anholt had very similar bunions. I believe Miss Anholt observed this as well.

Karen seemed to like wetting her toes, and she liked very much the hammock, when Miss Anholt pushed her high up and Karen screamed as if it was at a luna park.

HOLLY ANHOLT

Decision

NILS RECEDED FOR AWHILE from my dreams. A fresh starlet
assumed his prominence, though I never saw her face. Still, I
knew it was Karen, by the lake, in the woods, at the market in
the village. The faces were of old women in scarves, but behind
them, calling me, living in the trees and marshes like a sprite,
was a young girl, whispering things I could almost understand.
And there was another character, too, in the trees, stalking the
sprite, with a hideous, wizened face and foul red ass, a monkey
of my mind. This devil would have raped and robbed her. I
took him to be Heinz Schiessl.

Heinz Schiessl turned out not to look like this. He wore
large square glasses that old people get as part of their bifocal
package and that make everything else about a face look small.
His shirt collar was too large for him. His neck was stringy,
his little bit of hair was clipped neat and short, his glance was
slightly vacant. I know all this because I finally demanded a
meeting with him. What possessed me, all of that. I may have
been possessed only by my fear. I'd had so much fear lately
that it was growing intolerable, the way debt grows intolerable
for some people until they throw up their hands and declare
bankruptcy. I could have dealt with Schiessl as I'd dealt with
him before, by phone and lawyers. But now by night he was

stalking my sister. No way, sir. No way. Keep your filthy mitts off her. Have you no shame?

Though of course it was open to debate whose shame exactly I was thinking of when my mind thought such thoughts.

We met in Anja Mann's office. He was brought in by his son Richard, a man with a pinched-in nose who in all looked a little like a chipmunk and who I imagined could have been an accountant or minor civil servant. As I shook Heinz Schiessl's limp, arthritic hand, my own betrayed me with quiet trembling. I tried to remember what it was that desperation was supposed to breed. Invention? No, that was necessity. Maybe desperation just bred disaster. All I knew for certain was that if I was going to propose a second deal to the Schiessls, if I was going to be my father's daughter, fallen and redeemed as Nils said, I needed to be sure what I wanted out of it.

On the phone I had told Anja what that was: only Velden. She labored to dissuade me. Speculation in the Scheunenviertel was heating up. The city claim was close to the Oranienburgerstrasse. If I was only going to sell anyway, why not hold onto what was most valuable? It was then I told her that I was no longer thinking to sell. There'd been a couple seconds of telling silence on the phone after that.

She gave the Schiessls few details beyond my proposal. Heinz at first gave the impression of a Teutonic Sitting Bull, silent, stoic, inscrutable. Richard whispered in his ear a couple of times and still he sat there. I began to think he might be demented, but that wasn't actually the case. He may have been thinking about other things. He may have been thinking he was late for lunch. Who knew? But finally he was a stream of words, soft-spoken and a little high-pitched, and he asked his attorney Rosenthaler to translate, so that it would all be perfectly clear: "The city property is worth much more than the country property. We can't know at this time how much more. Are you sure you wish to do this?" When he finished speaking, he looked at me for perhaps the first and only time that day. It was an appraising look, steady and unafraid, but not a cruel one.

I duly nodded in answer to the question, the lawyers talked between themselves for quite a bit, and that was that, except that it wasn't quite that. The following day I received a call from the Schiessl son, inviting me for tea at the parents' house in Charlottenburg. He said his father had something to show me. I went because I couldn't think of a good enough reason not to.

It was a well-shaded stucco house in a quiet corner of Charlottenburg not far from the old Olympic Stadium. It turned out Heinz Schiessl was so pleased with the deal I'd made him that he wanted to thank me. We sat down for tea in the Schiessls' darkly furnished parlor, his invalid wife shuffling in as well with what I understood to be a nurse hovering. All of it felt a little like visiting a nursing home run by the Addams family. Grete. Grete was the wife's name.

"Bring the albums, Richard," Schiessl senior presently commanded. Soon Richard was placing two frayed leather bound photo albums in front of me. One of them had the German word for memories written in a sentimental, slanty script across its moldering cover. What a remarkable feeling it was to turn those album pages, akin to coming back to dinner at a house one had lived in for years, that strangers now owned. Photos of *their* summer house, *their* rowboat, *their* bit of the lake, all dutifully, efficiently marked "1938" or "1939" or "1940" with sometimes the month as well. I wanted to snatch it all back, as if to correct a cosmic mistake. But of course it wasn't a cosmic mistake. People mugging, people with their arms around each other, people in short-sleeves and squinting for the brightness of the summer day. One of the Schiessls was riding a horse. And then the point of the exercise: a number of the photographs were of other summer visitors, people who owned houses on either side and at other points on the lake. "Don't get hopes up," Heinz said. "I didn't know your parents. We dealt through lawyers. But perhaps others who summered there – who knows?" I began to take little mental notes, photo-graph by photograph, as the old man described whatever he remembered. We were near the end of the last album when he pointed to a photo of the far shore of the Moritzsee, where two houses were tucked into the trees. "This one," he pointed to the larger of the two. "Jews also. Until 1940, at least."

"Was that possible?" I asked.

"Before I entered the navy. They were there. Yes. Rosen."

"Yes? Rosen?" I asked.

He was sure. As well, he had a strong memory and he knew quite a lot about the Rosens, their business, their wealth, their relatives. They had only daughters, two daughters, but the brother of Rosen had a son. Franz? Yes of course, Franz. But the photos were only of the girls. I admitted nothing about already knowing Franz, or knowing that his uncle had a place on the lake. For some reason I didn't want to deflate their gesture. I didn't want to disappoint them.

Both of the old Schiessls claimed to know nothing about my parents hiding in the woods, or being caught there, or being even in the vicinity. Heinz was away in the navy, he said. Grete never went out to the country without him. I can't say that I believed them, but I did believe that I would never get them to say anything different.

I spent another few minutes, thanked everyone, and left, feeling very well-behaved, like a girl you can take anywhere.

GERTRUDE BAUM

Trust

I WAS NOT PREPARED for what came after Karen's visit, but I should have been. Miss Anholt didn't even tell me first, nor of course ask my judgment or if I would be aware of complications. No, I only heard it from her the next day. Miss Anholt had decided to give her claim to the Writers House to Karen. In a trust, if you please. Something to benefit Karen.

Now of course this was an act of generosity, so I could hardly point out to her that doing this would put Petra for sure in charge of the Writers House. No matter what they say, a "trust", in the end Petra would control everything. So I had gone from bad to worse. Miss Anholt was bad enough. But you see this is what my mother always said that my big heart would get me. More trouble than I could dream of. What will happen to me now? What will happen to any of us now?

I had only one chip left to play. This had to do with the question Miss Anholt was so eager to know: who betrayed her parents? As I wrote previously, I knew this person. It was all part of the story that I heard many years ago and that others knew as well. But what good would it do me to tell Miss Anholt? Would she suddenly stop giving the Writers House to Karen, would she think, oh no, it is really Mrs. Baum who is more deserving and Mrs. Baum has nowhere to go after twenty-four years? Of course not. I had only myself to blame for this whole pathetic "sister" business that I had no business sticking my nose in in the first place. What could I expect, that Miss Anholt would tell Petra, "The Writers House goes to Karen but you must keep Mrs. Baum on forever, and Mrs. Kirchner and Giessen to boot, or I will be very displeased?" What a joke. Miss Anholt said some such thing, in all events, or anyway she told me this, that she had said to Petra that Mrs. Baum should stay on. But do you imagine Petra will pay attention? Don't make me laugh until I choke. I would not work for Petra anyway. That would be absurd.

No, I didn't tell Miss Anholt who betrayed her parents. I saw no reason. As you have seen, it is too easy to cause too much trouble. Nor will I tell any of you. It is a matter of principle. But I am not afraid to give you hints. Why not? A good story wishes to be told. You see, it was not a matter of hating the Jews or kowtowing to the authorities. It was a matter of envy. There was one who was envious of Miss Anholt's father, for having Ute's affection, siring her child, giving her money, even for the fact that Ute helped him in the woods. This man was not Ute's later husband, either, that blockhead Jürg. It was someone else. I will not tell you who. I cannot. But I will give you one further clue. When Miss Anholt came to Velden, he was still alive. There. I've said enough. Please do not remind me that I began by saying I would tell you everything. One thing for certain I've found is that people do not always mean precisely what they say.

HOLLY ANHOLT

Call

ONE DAY HE CALLED. It was strange hearing his voice, after hearing it in my head for so long. The old story of living in shadows and coming out into the light. I listened to the little edges and burrs and almost didn't hear his words. I told him about Karen. It didn't surprise him. Nothing ever really surprised him. It was as though he had long ago decided that his life could not afford surprises, that it had enough on its plate with the already revealed.

I didn't want him to pity me. I wanted to make him laugh about something. So I said, "Why shouldn't Daddy have cast a few seeds like a proper lord of the manor?"

What a hearty, phony girl I must have sounded like then. I almost apologized. But he did laugh.

He asked me if we looked like each other at all. At first I said no, not really, I'd tried but couldn't find much, maybe just a hint of my father's soft chin, of his archy eyebrows that almost converged, and that made him look like he was concentrating even when he was dreaming.

Then I remembered our bunions.

I told Nils what I had done, or really was in the process of doing. My gift of blood and money, two things I didn't care to mix, it had nothing to do with goodness, he understood that, didn't he, I said. Just get rid of it, he said.

I was so glad to talk with him.

DAVID FÜRST

Love

YOU WOULD BE WELL ADVISED, if David Fürst says some-thing about love, to assume that the exact opposite is true. How can someone who knows nothing about something say something about it? Well, of course, people do so all the time. It is very probably the most common form of discourse.

I say the foregoing to mitigate my embarrassment. Nils is my dearest friend. This is so because he tolerates me, a more difficult task than those who know me less well might imagine. My feelings about his relations with the American girl are as follows:

1. I put aside my jealousy, as being virtually too banal to mention.
2. I believe that they will each continue to be very fond of each other, so that thirty or fifty years from now, or if some yokel starts talking about eternity, people will still be able to observe in them this fondness, no later love can or will take away this pentimento.
3. They were of course shadowed by their respective inheritances. This too is virtually too banal to mention.
4. Germany is a great country for Jews now, insofar as a Jew is not comfortable in life without a problem. Germany

and Israel, the two countries where Jews can truly have a problem. But see 3. above.

5. Romances falter not so much from exhaustion, but when one sees in the other something, as the divorce laws coyly put it, irreconcilable. Did such a thing appear in the mind of either? Here kindly note my unaccustomed modesty. I don't know.

6. Absence makes the heart grow fonder. Love flies away. A thousand cheap lyrics. (All of which are true the way clichés are always true, and many of which tend towards the implicit conclusion that just as there are some individuals who love better from afar or in secret, there are certain couples who realize without ever saying so that they see the other more clearly at a distance. All that is lost is a sense of touch. Everything else is more alive. Smiles are imagined.)

7. Mistakes, too, might have been made.

I might add to this list the tangential fact, perhaps already suggested in 1. above, that I became fond of the American girl. She seemed rather bland, at first, the way Americans tend to. But she could compete with us in every way. Easy to underestimate, so of course I did. Easy to bully, so of course I did. Later I began to feel ungainly in her presence, and haplessly overweight, like a character actor in an old, old movie.

FRANZ ROSEN

Consequences

NO ONE HAS SHUNNED ME. People have come up to me in
the street and embraced me and shed tears. This is the price
I have paid for not being such a hero after all. Berliners are
softies, I've discovered. Or at least they do not want anyone to
be too good.

FRANZ ROSEN

Alternatives

OR HOW DO I REALLY KNOW that such an optimistic scenario as I've just described is the truth? Or as they say in certain circles, the whole truth and nothing but the truth. A stranger's averted eyes on the bus, a friend who ends a phone conversation a shade too abruptly, a second or perhaps a third brandy after dinner – any of these are capable of catapulting me into darker imaginings.

Only to my personal knowledge has no one shunned me. Only some people have come up to me on the street and embraced me and shed tears. You may see the possible directions in which such qualifications may take me, either towards the shoals of paranoia or towards a more acute and candid apprehension of our human situation.

I would prefer not to dwell on it. If I am surrounded by people who secretly despise me, then I must cherish all the more those whose kindnesses are unmistakable. If people call me secret names, I must hold dear those names. I must vigilantly defend my optimism. It is only natural, in a climate such as ours, that people of ordinary capacity might hide their actual feelings if those feelings could subject them to public criticism or disgrace. A dearth of civic courage can work in any number of ways. Where it may once have paved the pathway to catastrophic events, today it may help to keep the peace. I do not know what others think. That is simply the truth, and perhaps a fortunate truth at that.

HEINZ SCHIESSL

Defeat

WHAT'S FAIR IS FAIR. I have always said this. I tried to explain this to Miss Anholt. I paid twice for her father's properties. Once, alright, perhaps not enough. Although who knows? Who can say? There were general laws that disabled the Jews. Once these laws were passed, then of course the value of a Jew's interest in a property would be reduced. You talk about markets. This was the market. Did I take advantage of the market? It is a market's nature to be taken advantage of. Is this not what the Anglo-Americans are always telling us? But, alright, leaving aside this fine point. Perhaps in 1938 I paid not enough. Perhaps I received a bargain based on Mr. Anholt's exigent position. But after the war, whose position was exigent? Mine, of course. We were bombed and impoverished. Whereas he was helped in many ways, for sure, to start anew in the richest country on earth. You cannot tell me he wasn't helped. I don't know the details but of course he must have been. I, of course, could not have gone to California. I would have been put in a camp. And yet, to clear the record, again I paid. I wanted no arguments that I was a Nazi beast, a predator. I paid liberally. Of course the sum will seem to you piddling today. But in our ruined city then, it was, believe me, a good sum, an act of faith. Even Anholt told me this, through his lawyer.

It was a very fair sum. And if I may say, through my limited personal affairs with him, Anholt himself was a fair-minded man, much as I hold myself to be. We had this in common. I am not ashamed of it. Then within two years of my payment to him, the Communists took it all from me, the city property, the country property, all of it, without a dime in compensation. These were the true criminals, not I.

Now it is 1990, the Communists are done, and comes Miss Anholt. She wants her property back. All very well, the law provides for it, except for one thing: it is not hers, or even her father's – her father sold it fairly to me! Who in turn lost it to the Red thugs. But if anyone should get it back from the Red thugs, it is surely me, not her. But the law does not allow it. I was expropriated too early, when the Russians were still occupying, when the GDR had not yet been established. The German law does not concern Russian expropriations, only those of its lackeys. What to do? I thought very hard on this. I exercised my faculty for fair play. I realized that if Miss Anholt and I could become partners, we could both be winners after all. I thought I had been very clever. Of course it is the case that if I had never presented my deed and contract at all, then Miss Anholt could likely have sailed through on her claim uncontested. But what fairness would there have been in that? My representative explained this to her. Like her father, I too have children. Do they deserve nothing? Am I simply to throw their best interests off the roof? But you see at first she was one of these Americans who can only see Nazi, Nazi, Nazi, as if this one word made a bright explosion that destroyed everything else about a person or situation. I pet my dog, I pay my rent. But never mind. I see that for even these, by the person intent on it, I can be accused. All I wish to say is that Miss Anholt came around eventually. She came down from her moral heights. For this I was quite grateful, actually. We then had a deal. We would become partners. And I must tell you something more: there is nothing that thrills me more than when two parties who had once been enemies reach an agreement based on reason and shared interest. This is true cooperation. It is touching to me, that Miss Anholt and I could cooperate. I love this when I see such things in films, and I love it even more in life. People looking past their grievances. This is what life is about.

You will say, and I'm afraid quite properly, that if we had not been defeated, I would not now be trumpeting the virtues of cooperation so enthusiastically. But we were defeated. This is the essential point. In defeat I learned many things. It is one of the best teachers, as those who have been defeated will sometimes tell you. I was particularly moved when Miss Anholt on her own initiative proposed that she receive the country property and we the city lots. She took a financial sacrifice here, in favor of sentiment. I was particularly impressed by this. It was on this account that I invited her to tea. Our family had photographs from our time in Velden which I thought might be useful or interesting for her to see. I must say, she was fascinated by them. Of course there was some oddness, as there always is when one sees another enjoying what you had known as your own home. This was the case even though Miss Anholt had never lived in Velden. She seemed to have absorbed a strong connection through studying her parents' pictures. And so to see my father on a horse in front of her parents' cottage, as if he were a Cossack just arrived from the steppe! I could appreciate her anxiety. She seemed to an equal degree animated by certain pictures of one of the other families on the lake, the Rosens, who like the Anholts were present until the war. In particular she lingered over a photograph of the Rosens' nephew, whose name she perhaps recognized. He is a rather well-known local invert who lied about his past during the war. I find it more than a little dismaying that his confession of cowardice, which appeared not so long ago in the papers, seems to have made him more popular than ever, at least in certain quarters.

More recently I've heard that Miss Anholt gave away her claim. Rosenthaler the lawyer heard this. A family case, a charity situation. Now if she was doing charity, fine, why didn't she give it to me! Only joking, of course. But this was a little rich, to hear this. First she fights, then she doesn't fight. An odd girl. I respect her for it, of course. Though I suspect, as well, that she must be so well-settled financially that the property meant nothing to her in those terms.

Now I care to make some more general comments. Go ahead, stop up your ears, blind your eyes. But I will be heard, somewhere! I mentioned previously that I had found the experience of defeat educational. But not everything I have learned would you classify as cozy or warm-hearted.

For instance, every fair-minded person will agree in principle that when there is a crucial battle, the victor declares the history. Victor's rules, everyone says it. But with respect to the World War, no one of the victors, ever, says such a thing, or takes a discount on the received truths based on the likelihood that victor's rules are in operation. If the National Socialists had found a cure for cancer, surely it would be declared today that the cure was secretly to make people sick. Not one single virtue of the regime or the time is ever applauded. Even the origin of the People's Car is forgotten. And if you remind others how odd this is, how similar it is, in spirit, to the ancient practice of salting the ruins of an enemy so that nothing will ever grow there again, they will mock you. Believe me, I have seen the movies. They are very funny. I am not afraid to laugh.

And why is all of this? The mass murder of the Jews, of course. But not the act of mass murder itself, rather the possibility that if all that ever touched the mass murder or might be considered to be related to it is not anathematized utterly, it might recur. I understand this. But it is an insufficient explanation. If it were a sufficient explanation, then those who annihilated the American red man would be similarly anathematized, or those whose colonial practices decimated native populations the world over or perhaps even those who dropped atomic bombs or fire bombs on people. No, it is simply a case of victor's rules.

But why should I even bother to say what can only cause me trouble? Because I am an old man, for sure. I do not condone the killing of the Jews for one minute. Even in the war I knew perfectly well that not all Jews were Bolshevik animals or Wall Street bankers manipulating Roosevelt or lewd theatrical producers seducing our women. Even during the war, with death all around and on every front, I found what I heard, in rumors and whispers, to be shocking, disturbing, even unbelievable. You will of course jump and say that when I use the word "unbelievable" I am somehow excusing myself. I make no excuse. The word is only what it is. Blood is on my hands. I have made such amends as I might, as for instance with my affairs with Miss Anholt's father. But part of my amends are to say the truth now, despite all victor's rules. The world faces problems that are very nearly insuperable. I will not impose on you the banality of naming them, because every thinking man knows them. All that differs among thinking men is their ordering of the magnitude of the catastrophes that await us. I ask very simply: is it worthwhile, in service of victor's rules or mental sloth or political convenience, to sow with salt every idea or association or instinct or art that ever found favor with a political tradition that matured in our mid-century crises but that had its roots, obviously and profoundly, in the most ancient civilizations?

If I could say, it was the madness, the intoxication, the excess, of our leaders that brought catastrophe and evil. They were like the worst emperors, like a string of Caligulas and Neros. And it was our fault, as a nation, to be seduced by them, and in our seduction to confuse them with Augustus and Hadrian. This is one more lesson that defeat has well-taught me.

But please observe how it brings me back to Miss Anholt. Do I hate Jews? I am not fond of Jews, on average. I would say that I share in the common prejudices, having had these inflamed, for certain, during the National Socialist period, then mooted by the subsequent revulsion, then allowed by the passage of time to slowly re-seed, so that once again I am all-in-all what might be called a typical, quiet anti-Semite, with a belief that Jews control too much and so on but with qualified support for the State of Israel, as all-in-all the best solution to the Jewish Question which I believe is fruitless for any truly rational man to deny. There. Have I blackened my name in certain circles sufficiently for one day? But those certain circles would of course never have heard of me anyway. I do not count. I am too little. Yet I grew quite fond of Miss Anholt. Her pleasant demeanor, her modesty, and so on, notwithstanding the oddness which I previously mentioned, and which was perhaps attributable to the oddness of the situation in which she found herself, the insecurity and unfamiliarity, even, perhaps, the morbidity. She may have imagined she was making a pact with the Devil. Ah yes, even with Goethe looking over her shoulder!

I should only have wished to get to know her better. I might have put her better at ease. We might have had interesting conversations. Only a dullard would see a contradiction here. If there were more Jews around, it's quite possible more would be my friends. Though I don't believe this is wise national policy, more Jews, more Turks, more everybody. It is simply the way things are. Victor's rules. Catastrophe. But you see, I am a fairminded person. I have no wish to be irritating simply for irritation's sake. I seek a world such as I once had with Miss Anholt, of cooperation and shared interest. People looking past their grievances. This is what life is about.

PETRA LUESCHER

Gift

YOU DON'T IMAGINE for a minute that Karen liked her fresh new sister better on account of this so-called "gift" of hers. Why should she? She had no need of it. She was perfectly well taken care of already. She had everything she needed. If she so much as spat, I cleaned up the spit. If she soiled her bed, I washed the sheets.

I am not impressed. I don't give a good goddamn. That woman can have all the money in the world and do whatever she wants with it and it would make no difference to me. Comes in here, acts like a big shot. Well of course. What a lot of garbage. Lording it over an imbecile, is that something a grown woman should be proud of? Of course Karen doesn't love her. Do you know who she loves? That idiot on television. The one I'm constantly spending postage so that she can collect more stupid photographs of him. That's what we're dealing with, that's what I'm up against. I've raised her my whole life. But who cares what I think anyway? The sister who has nothing. Well I'll tell you something, I don't have to have anything to know what's right. There are ways for people to behave, maybe they don't teach that in California but over here we're not impressed, even Karen. You know what she said to me? "Do I have to go see my sister again?" And not only that. "Is she really my sister?" She doesn't even believe this fairy tale. Ute was no virgin, you know. My mother danced around, to put it politely. Who knows? I'm not saying no, I'm simply saying we don't know who the father was for sure. What if Ute was only telling this Anholt things in order to get his money? That would be a good one, wouldn't it? Her moron daughter finally gets it. And Petra, what does Petra get, Petra whose own father was quick enough out the door, oh Petra can do the wash and shut up. Well not this time. Believe me. This time I'm getting something. It's only right. My whole life. My whole life, and what thanks have I got? Petra, turn the TV on. Petra, I can't hear the sound now. Petra this, Petra that, one thing after the other.

I'll say something else. I don't care if you like it or not. Karen wouldn't even step foot in that house. She's happy where she is. Who do these people think we are? We were getting along perfectly fine without them. I had to drag her even once. "Oh come on, Karen, let's go see, your very kind sister has invited us to her beautiful house on the lake with many rooms and wonderful things!"

"I hate my sister," she said. Those were her very words. "I hate my sister."

"That's not right," I said to her. "To hate your sister. Why? Don't do such a thing."

"Because you're my sister," she said.

"But you can have more than one, you know."

"I don't want more than one."

There. So no one can accuse me of poisoning anyone's mind. I didn't poison Karen's mind. This was her opinion from the start. I was perfectly suitable. Those were my exact words. "That's not right, to hate your sister."

It did no good. Even after the sister gave us everything, Karen still didn't wish to see her anymore. People say she's an imbecile, Karen, but certain things she can certainly see.

Nor will I tell you my exact plans for the place. If I sell it, I sell it, it's none of your goddamn business. If I want to go to Phuket, that's none of your business either. Are you going to accuse me of taking a vacation? I'll take any vacation I want to. No one can tell me I don't deserve a vacation. That's the problem. Everybody has an opinion. Everybody butts into other people's business. No one knows what really went on. No one knows how I've spent my life.

Karen is a sweet girl. She just wants to be left alone with her television. She thinks one day the idiot on the television, Hunter, his name is Hunter and he is also from California, is going to find her and marry her. Then her life will be complete.

People have many ideas why all this happened. I am referring to the so-called "gift." One is that this woman had so much money she didn't know what else to do with it, it all meant nothing to her, it was like crumbs off her plate. Another is that people are always saying how we must be guilty about the Jews but I don't even know a Jew and this was the opposite exactly, the Jew felt guilty for coming in here and disturbing our lives the way she did. Another is that she was as big an imbecile as Karen. Another is that she was deeply touched and all of that, she loved her sister, all of that, she was so happy to find a sister, all of that. This last explanation I don't believe one bit. Who was she trying to kid?

HOLLY ANHOLT

Demonstration

SHE SAT ON A ROCK with her sign on the muddy ground near her feet. A few people had flashlights but mostly it was dark. We were somewhere in the countryside, not far from the city, having arrived in motley cars strewn around like lumps of coal, darker than the night. Beyond us were the barracks of the asylum-seekers. We caught glimpses of their lives, men in underwear, women with wash, the stark, tinny light of a television. Curtains blew through open windows. It was a quiet moment on the new front that had opened, between the asylum-seekers and those who didn't want them in the country.

I suppose you would say we were there to keep the peace. Schoolteachers and lawyers and students and solid citizens, responding to Anja Mann's call: "We have to say to them: no. Now. Before it starts to flame up big. In particular, to show these Eastern police that there's a price also if they ignore the problem." Though I wasn't there for such noble reasons. I was there because this was my lawyer's other life, which I'd managed to know about only as rumor, and I was curious, and felt a little bit obliged, like somebody who's been to somebody's house for dinner several times and has never asked to see the beautiful garden. Nor did I think Simona was there to be altruistic either. It was more a reflex with Simona. Tell her about a demonstration and she would come.

But on this cold night there was something more. Simona was lying in wait. She was like a beggar in the shadows. From her rock she watched Anja march here and there, checking lists, bucking up spirits, giving orders, courting the waning interest of the TV people – whatever might be done in the dead spots by the captain of an undertaking such as ours. In the darkness we could make out little, but Anja was so upright, with her top-knot of hair and prominent nose, as if some mad Prussian geneticist in search of civic courage had attempted a cross between a samurai and Charles de Gaulle, that the faintest shadow of her was unmistakable. When Anja disappeared altogether, Simona resembled a bored, disconsolate child, her chin resting in her hand or her foot making idle circles in the muddy dirt.

And then Anja would reappear, like a looming ocean liner out of an old movie's fog, and Simona would follow her with her eyes. Beseeching glances, knowing glances, helpless glances; a full repertory of pleading, to all of which Anja was immune. Though it was possible, as well, that she hadn't even noticed Simona sitting on that rock, or seen her name on the sign-in sheet. But I didn't believe it; Anja was too organized for that, too in control. She was one of those for whom survival must have meant scanning the horizon.

A conversation that never took place:

Forgive me, my queen, but I only wrote notes until 1983, I only wrote notes for two years and a half, I only pointed out your Zionist tendencies twice.

Forget it, my lowly subject, whose nose properly touches the ground, my slave, unworthy and pathetic, whom I wouldn't forgive in ten thousand lives, who is only telling me this now because it will come out anyway, who would still keep it secret if she could, who only got that place in the Writers Union house to write a fatuous, self-serving autobiography by ratting me out.

It never took place because Anja wouldn't allow it to. At last Simona got up from her rock and went over to where Anja was talking with others in a circle. She loitered at the periphery until there was room for her to elbow in, then stood in silent hope that her relentlessness would soon pay off. Others drifted away. "Anja..." Perhaps she got that far. I couldn't hear but I could see Anja turn away from the circle. Was it at the exact moment Simona spoke or caught her glance? Simona followed her and touched Anja's sleeve, a shadow puppet's gesture. Anja pulled her arm away.

Simona came back to her rock and her sign. Sometime before she had told me she was leaving Berlin for Jerusalem. Now wasn't that nice news, I had thought, but didn't say, afraid that if I showed any support for the idea, she might reconsider. She was gripping the handle of her sign with both hands now, as if it were her last friend, she and her sign taking on the world. But the cardboard part of it still dragged in the mud. "*Asyls* in! Nazis out!" Perhaps it was my mother's pity that I kept feeling for Simona; if you ask, you shall be forgiven, the world according to Doe. And why not, what was wrong with that, wasn't that the only way the world would ever work?

And Anja Mann, heroic leader of the old GDR dissidents, now left without much of a portfolio, rooting around for the next evil thing? What was wrong with her, that she couldn't forgive two years in jail, slanders, family suffering, psychiatric tortures, loss of health? I felt like a fool that night. I was confused and I hated to be confused. Simona had a few tears, as well. I hated her tears. It was some moments after she produced them that I went after Anja, not ostentatiously, but in Simona's plain sight, as if I were sick of hiding some stupid thing. We spoke for a minute or so. She thanked me for coming. When I arrived back in the shadows, Simona asked me, "So you know her?"

"Anja?"

"You know her quite well."

"She's been my lawyer. With the claims."

"I should have guessed," Simona said. The words, of course, of a woman who's just discovered the identity of her husband's lover.

"Sorry," I said.

But I offered no further explanation, nor did she ask for one. A stalemate of little lies.

Later the skinheads came. From the back of the shelter we heard a window break and then shouting. We jumped up, grabbing our signs as though they were weapons. Our signs, our brave defense against the rock-throwers. We raced around to the back of the barracks and tried to form a line. It was all fairly chaotic and exciting and never seemed particularly dangerous. Inside the barracks men in t-shirts ran from window to window. Whoever had flashlights shone them into the woods, trying to catch glimpses of the attackers. There couldn't have been many. I caught glimpses of two or three, advancing or retreating, as shadowy as guerrillas. A couple more windows broke. The skins disappeared into the woods. Later I would learn that two of the boys from David's car workshop were among the attackers, but I saw none of their faces that night. Anja's demonstration made the evening news.

FRANZ ROSEN

List

Beerman, Felix, 1887–1915
Beerman, Siegfried, 1894–1916
Beerman, Walter, 1890–1915
Mayer, Isador, 1891–1918
Rosen, Hugo, 1886–1914
Rosen, Julius, 1881–1918
Rosen, Louis, 1888–1914
Rosen, Max, 1891–1915
Schlösser, Artur, 1897–1915
Schlösser, Ernst, 1882–1916
Silber, Willy, 1895–1916

So there it is, the list that I never thought I would make. The list, even, that I may have called barbaric. But I suppose it was always in my mind. More recently I have stayed up late with record books and family albums, fretting, deducing, counting. You may imagine that it was a sleepless devotion, conceived in shame and doubt. Of the 12,000 or so Jewish men who died fighting for Germany in the Great War, it seems that these eleven were my blood relations. What pride, what sadness, too. Sadness even that I should do such a thing, make such a list, a man with my history, a man over seventy years old. They say, about such matters as the Shoah, that we must never forget. But there are others things that must never be forgotten as well.

ANJA MANN

Justice

IT WOULD BE UNETHICAL for me to speak about the cases
of any of my clients. In particular I wish to emphasize that
my comments below in no way derive from the claim of Miss
Holly Anholt. But if you only read the newspapers, you would
hear of claims where the capitalist lottery is on full display,
where distant relations receive windfalls of tens of millions,
where institutions such as even state art museums acquiesce
to flimsy claims, ostensibly because they fear adverse public
relations if they fight, but more likely because they understand
that an expensive private sale of the claimed painting would
boost the value of their remaining holdings of the same artist
beyond measure. A new class of greedy and sanctimonious
lawyers, particularly in America, has been nourished as well,
and this can never be a good thing.

Thus a certain ambivalence has crept into my feelings about
the claims process taken as a whole. On the one hand stands
the obvious justice supporting the vast majority of persons
who have filed claims. They once owned property, the property
was taken from them by coercive means without fair compensation, and now that the totalitarian regimes which supported
such unjust takings are gone, why shouldn't they have their
property back? Many such persons are less interested in the

material gain to be had from their filing than in making some small gesture – small as against the murders and exiles that accompanied the loss of mere property – towards the reestablishment of justice. Here I speak not only of justice in the present tense, but justice that recognizes an historical past, that seeks continuity with it. Moreover, provided proofs are forthcoming and legitimacy is established, our laws provide for such claims. It cannot be said juridically that there is anything unjust in pursuing rights that are nothing more than what the law provides for.

On the other hand, there is the less refined justice supporting those who might be dispossessed or whose lives might otherwise be disrupted by the claims process. Their numbers in truth may be relatively small. But their crime, in such cases as exist, is of course typically no more than bad luck. They relied, just as the earlier dispossessed ones did, on discredited arrangements, on a supplanted regime.

Nor is it possible, as a general rule, for one to judge regarding the relative emotional and economic interests of both types of parties, the earlier dispossessed and the now-perhaps-to-be dispossessed.

Moreover it is a simple fact of history that property has regularly changed hands as the result of theft, warfare, and lies. Radical regime changes have everywhere been accompanied by changes in property ownership. "Just compensation", historically speaking, is hardly a reliable thing. Thus trying to sort things out back to the Nazi time is rather like spitting into a sea wind. While we're at it, why not go back to the Thirty Years War? Then everyone would be uncertain of everything. Actually, I rather like this idea. It might be the final revenge of Karl Marx.

Finally, while properly speaking we ought pay it no mind whatever, nonetheless it is so that these property claims in the hands of the right demagogue have the potential to stir unwholesome sentiments in the citizenry, even as today we face already a rising tide of other social problems engendered by reunification. Some days I feel like I only have two hands.

Perhaps as a GDR schoolgirl, I read a definition of Greek tragedy which suggests that at its core is an irreconcilable clash between two competing social goods. In this regard, there may yet be a dollop of tragedy woven into the fabric of some of these property claims. One part tragedy, one part monkey business, one part justice.

I am not unmindful of the irony involved in a lawyer such as myself schooled in the Eastern ideology now making her living in defense of private property. Nonetheless, I am grateful for the honest work the claims process has provided me.

NILS SCHREIBER AND DAVID FÜRST

Comanches

Nils:

My favorite place in the city isn't there anymore. The Potsdamer Platz isn't what it used to be. It used to be a Cold War frontier. It used to be a weedy, bombed-out wasteland where kids lived in the back of trucks getting stoned all day waiting for the millennium and there was one ramshackle Turkish café out-of-doors with broken chairs to sit on and a construction crane from which for a few marks you could bungee-jump. I don't know what happened to that crane. It may have been used to build one of the corporate towers that stand there now. The kids were waiting for the millennium because according to the logic of their lives something miraculous was supposed to happen then.

My son Erich was one of those kids. He lived there from when he was seventeen. He was dark and mopey like his mother and he had soft eyes and, yes, I was proud enough of him, being out there, taking his chances. Every time I saw him I thought what a big, goofy question mark he was. Once again the world could be anything. His stoned mysticism gave way to stoned politics, and he became a Comanche, one of the anarchist groups that fought the police in Kreuzberg every weekend and half the time won. I got him his first job on the old Potsdamer Platz, eighty marks to jump off the crane and write it up for the paper. The angle being, as Erich put it, Mr. Average Degenerate Citizen Goes For It. He got the jump paid for too. It was another one of those half-breathless moments when it looked like the paper was about to go belly up and I thought if I didn't get him a chance soon, I'd never be able to give him one at all. But the paper is still around and Erich survived the jump and his article was pretty good, he got the rush and the fall and every bounce, though he never wrote another one. Of course he doesn't live on the Potsdamer Platz anymore.

David:

My dear friend Nils neglected to mention that there was also an old MiG fighter that lay among the trucks, ruined, scavenged, and graffitied by the kids. Personally that MiG was my favorite part, because you could climb in the cockpit and because of the mess the kids made of it. The Ozymandias of the no man's land, the Cold War's freakiest emblem.

My dear friend Nils also neglected to mention that it was his son Erich's Comanches who firebombed my car workshop. How did I know this? It wasn't so hard. They left a note that said, "We the Comanche faction of *Autonome* gives fair warning. By the destruction of the so-imagined ironic skin car project, we announce: fascists, beware, next time we set fire to your bodies, and you can burn in a hell on earth!" It was the end of the shop.

I never reported them to the police. What would have been the point? I was sick of the shop by then, and so were my charges, and we were sick of each other. Her Stuffiness Anja Mann had come to me to complain that two of my boys had been involved in an attack on an asylum-seekers' barracks. I preferred to deny this, because it was blatantly against all the rules I'd set up, but once again, as in the matter of the fire-bombing, the proof was not utterly dismissible: she had a dark but clear photograph of Johann and Hermann running off, even wearing the shirts with our shop's name on it. Wear the shirt to a pogrom, you shits! Some people never learn. I would include myself in this last statement.

So the Comanches did us a favor. The world works as it should. After a lively physical combat, in which one of them broke my nose and I managed to inflict a bit of damage myself, I duly wrote up the story of my boys and the final failure of my efforts to reform them in a more capitalistic mode, just as they predicted I would. As they would be quick to point out, only one of us got paid. I am not sorry that it was me. I was broke.

Self-disgust took its usual back seat.

Nils:

It was also where I met Holly for the last time, sitting on the least-broken folding chairs we could find, sipping our coffee, the crane hovering over us, under a long gray sky. She wasn't ready to leave Berlin yet, but she was getting closer. Thinking about jobs, thinking about places. No longer the real estate queen of Velden, no longer the plucky adventurer. Not that she was ever exactly either of those, but surely she feared that she was.

We talked about Franz Rosen, as we so often did, as if he were the secret cypher that linked us. I told her about my rage, how I'd been in a rage towards him for weeks after I interviewed him. She wanted to know why. Holly, my love, the eternal straight man. Because I felt seduced by him (I said), made a fool of, and the rage came when I realized I kind of liked it.

Then she took a small brown envelope out of her jacket pocket and pushed it my way. Inside was a pin with a sky blue background, a few Cyrillic letters, and an antique fighter plane manned by a tiny man in goggles. It was an old Soviet aviator's pin, she said, an airman first class pin, that she had bargained off a hustler near Checkpoint Charlie, near my office. She was quite proud of it and I loved her for being quite proud of it. Genuine, no counterfeit, yeah sure, she said. But she thought I might like the blue sky background. I did. It was like the sky in Oksana's paintings.

David:

Friendships need never be explained. But if I had to do it, if some dragon with claws and a tongue of fire stood over us and our lives depended on it, I would say the friendship of Nils and myself had to do with a shared understanding: that beneath the fine rebuilding of our city there was the whiff of unburied bodies, or improperly buried bodies. But what to do about it, morbidity not being an entirely acceptable option? A friendship arising from a quandary.

OKSANA KOSLOVA

Brushstrokes
(from her notebooks)

Franz Rosen: *the coming of evening in dark blue – the name of a rose, Duchesse de Brabant or Souvenir de la Malmaison – a regrettable forgetfulness – a figure in a film, overweight and a little shabby from lack of sleep, lovestruck – fingers on a pocket watch*

Nils Schreiber: *violence – Christ on the cross – sweet reason – a worn leather jacket*

Herbert Kaminski: *a peacock that has lost its feathers, wandering around on a vast lawn*

David Fürst: *a salesman with samples – brown shoes – saliva and hope*

Simona Jastrow: *a schoolgirl's plaid skirt and white socks – a shriveled peach on a sill – a notebook – violets*

Mischa Lander: *beaks, birds of prey, men with hooded falcons, Horus – fluorescent lights, iron rooms – Eros in chains, screaming bloody murder – white sideburns, gaunt cheeks – a boy fallen in a well – rain in the afternoon*

Anja Mann: *a glass of water – stone steps – sturdy shoes – a cape that covers her mouth like a veil and that causes her, unexpectedly and unseen by others, to smile*

Holly Anholt: *a flying flag – a small boat, brightly painted – Chagall, the shtetl – the undeniability of luck displayed as allegory – freshly baked sweets – dark curls – forest animals in dreams*

Self-portrait: *lost causes – little pools of light – skin and bones*

HOLLY ANHOLT

Mourning

THE DICTIONARY SAYS THAT MOURNING is the expression of grief, and that grief is deep mental anguish, as for a loss. I know the dictionary definition because I looked it up once. I can't remember when I did this, but all my life I've looked up things in the dictionary that I didn't understand. My father died and my mother died, but I never really mourned. I remembered them fondly and went on, perhaps the dictionary definition like a placeholder to remind me of what was missing. I said this once to Nils, then added in my embarrassed fashion that I was probably being dramatic. He listened and said I wasn't. I didn't believe him then.

What brought me to Velden? A bit of black-and-white film, my mother's wariness, secrets. No. Something missing in myself, something unaccounted for, something which in the middle of my mostly normal life I couldn't say. It doesn't seem so different from the world as a whole, now that I put it in such bare, poor terms. And yet this would have been my wish, if I could have put it into words: to rejoin the human race.

Nor could I have told you if you'd asked me if there were more like me than not; more people in the world who feel they don't belong, or more who feel they do.

Out of touch, living in a fog, a little bit confused.

Having a boyfriend while in a fog, something that sounds like a misdemeanor, spelled out in a municipal code.

But you can live in a fog and not know it, you can blame it on the world, you can believe the world itself is hard to see, as it was yesterday, as it is today, as it will be the day you die.

I always felt at home in fog. I remember spending two weeks in Mendocino when the fog never went away and I never really wanted it to. I wore a raincoat and pretended I was many things. It was only on the day I was to leave that I woke up wishing for sunlight.

After making my grand gesture, giving the place to Karen, I wanted nothing but to leave Velden, yet I didn't. I had hoped that gesture would free me from all of it, the place, my mother's claim, my parents' silence, my failed affair. But grand gestures, I learned, don't always work the way they're supposed to. They can leave you feeling empty and theatrical, as if the very structures of your mind were sets to strike.

And once the sets are struck, what is left?

My bits of film, which I looked at every day. My sister in her baby carriage, the fadedness of the image, the ephemeral atmosphere it created. We leave such little traces of ourselves. A photograph seems to say, *our* lake, *our* sunlight, *our* happiness, as if the possessive pronoun would be there forever. A first, lovely mistake.

And my parents. How easily now I could see the distance between them which I had never seen before. Sitting within arm's length of the TV night after night, because the remote for the VCR was lost, running my bit of tape back and forth, stopping always at the moment of the two of them by the lakefront posing for the camera, together but not touching, so that you could see a jagged white slice of the lake between the outlines of their clothes. It seemed the largest thing in the frame now, that white slice of nothing.

This place of my parents' happiness, this Camelot, this idyll, this whatever it was in space and time, where they thought they were safe and assimilated and a little lazy and together, or *I* thought they were safe and assimilated and a little lazy and together...like normal people...like happy people...but history is there to be revised.

I decided to return to the bunker. There, I felt, would be something more like fact. How could it have been otherwise, with Ute, Karen's mother, coming around? The truths of their lives laid bare and then an heroic struggle for survival. Who could deny them that much? I wished only to touch it. I wished only to feel for one moment some true connection to the lives that were theirs before I was born. It had not been in this house in Velden, it had certainly not been in Auschwitz. Or anyway I hadn't found it. Maybe blame it all on me.

I went alone this time. Two shovels, gloves, water, a hat. A vague idea where I was going. It was a day early in summer, every tree in leaf, the forest floor damp and soft as if newborn, a day you could sweat in the shade just walking around. The key to finding the bunker, I knew, was how unnatural it looked, like a lump, like some big creature that had hunkered down and thrown dirt and leaves and roots on itself for camouflage. I had watched Mrs. Baum's steps closely enough, at least on our exit. I knew where we came out, at a bend on the Velden-Karlsheim road. So that's where I went in. I left myself two hours to find it and two hours to find my way out, being afraid of darkness and bears. Bears, very funny. Cartoon wolves, even funnier. A few squirrels were more like it. After an hour and a half of aimlessness, down this path, down that one, crossing back on the same path twice or three times, I stumbled into the clearing of buttercups. And there was my hunkered-down thing.

Whatever digging I'd done before was invisible by now, covered over with late spring profusion. I dug with abandon for awhile, slashing and jabbing with my shovel, pulling away vines with my hands, then I tired. I sat, rested, and resumed more slowly, as if I'd learned a lesson and would now be prudent. In it for the long haul, I would strip this concrete animal bare and dig out its insides until I found what I was looking for.

And what was that? Some scrap, some proof, some remainder of any sort of three people's lives that were lived here long ago. Something to take home, I suppose, a souvenir, a proof, no, anything at all.

Or it had nothing to do with a thing. I would simply dig myself to exhaustion, I would see, but what would I see, you don't just see things that aren't there. My parents' lives, Martin, Doe, Helena, as if in some bizarre application of thesis-antithesis-synthesis the result would somehow be me fully formed, fully alive.

The heat of the day increased and everything went still more slowly. Criticism more usual to my sleepless hours before dawn crept into my thoughts. Epiphanies were for phonies, archaeology was no substitute for life. Why didn't I just blow the thing up? Why didn't I hire someone else to dig? Why did I ever leave Paris? What was wrong with me, anyway? And as a counterpoint to my criticism, I dug.

I hung my jacket on a branch. There was too much overgrowth, the shovel couldn't cut it, I needed shears, which I didn't have. I stripped away the easy stuff, made little dents in the earth, grew little piles of dirt on every side of it, but still the bunker sat there like a half-buried sphinx, its true shape obscure.

I dug and thought of Nils, his narrow twinkling eyes, the low ironic rush of his insight, his reticence, that left room for my own.

I dug and thought of my father and all his Oldsmobiles, I tried to remember them each in order, which came after which, which had fins and which were Rocket 88's with those little rocket emblems, and what colors they were.

Or never mind those, what about this, my father and the Nazi cutting a deal, me and the Nazi cutting a deal.

Keeping my mind in order, keeping the world in order, continuing to dig. I hit layers of composted leaves and removed them, then began discovering bits of tar paper from what might have been a roof. Then there were chunks of concrete, and from the inside out I began to find the outlines of the walls. I excavated, hauling concrete away with the dirt. And I thought of Franz Rosen in his haberdasher's coal bin in Prenzlauer Berg. But did I find my mother's wedding band? No, of course not. My father's pipe? Hardly. An old button that could have been from his jacket? No. An arm off my sister's doll? No. A battery from their flashlight? No. Nothing like any of that.

Again I stepped back to see what I had accomplished, but because I'd removed so much debris to the outside, the shape of the bunker appeared scarcely clearer than before. It seemed confused, as though it had been disturbed but to no particular purpose, as though by some ignorant creature simply bent on a bit of destruction.

I drank more water. I resolved to turn the bowl that I had dug in the middle of the bunker into something cleaner, closer to the walls, more thorough, more like a cube.

Again I picked up my shovel. I suddenly felt as though I were leaping into a grave.

Who was to judge what any of this was about?

I struggled to remember why I had begun. And where I had begun.

What a terrible waste was my life, I thought. What a terrible waste was this hole.

I found the digging more difficult, the forest floor hotter, my muscles more fatigued.

It was as though I were digging towards an impossibility. My mind turned hazy and dim.

Something tinkled in my ears.

The end of the line, came a dizzy voice.

In my mother's arms, warm milk before sleep.

Ha ha, ha ha, ha ha, ha ha, don't you be going insane before your hole is dug. Not until you find your mommy and daddy.

I dug my way to a corner of the bunker and scraped the slab walls until the corner was clear and defined. Job well done, came a dizzy voice, there's no reason in the world why this corner should be so clean and defined but you wanted it that way. You wanted something your way. This was your house, after all. This was where your parents lived. And Helena. Was she just like you?

Later I knew that I'd begun to float away even before I found it. My heart was a hot air balloon. My muscles were ground to bone. *Arbeit macht frei*. Ha ha, ha ha, ha ha, give a nice hand, ladies and gentlemen, for the bitter old joke that won't quit.

No one would ever find me here. No one could ever find me here.

Unless I was given away by a little piece of paper, a sliver of paper, pushing out of the dirt in the corner of the bunker.

Announce yourself, intruder! Are you some kind of spy? There's spies around here, don't you know.

I put my shovel aside and knelt by my discovery. I had a penknife. I dug gingerly around the sliver. It was something. There was more of it. There was thickness. There were pages of it.

I revived and dug with my fingers. Half of a page emerged, and then another half-page, old and soggy and fragile. I pulled half a magazine out of the dirt, then quickly the other half. Thinking immediately of Nils, of how I would show it to him, this thing that I had found, *Nils, look, this something from my parents' lives.*

Then I saw the cover. It was a GDR magazine on cheap newsprint that looked ancient enough but was dated April 11, 1973, with a faded sepia photo of the Leningrad Symphony Orchestra on the front.

I sank down and stared at the magazine. For a moment I wondered how it got there. Someone on a tryst, or someone catching a snooze, or someone on the lam? And why did I think of a shepherd? Shepherds didn't live in forests. Shepherds lived in fairy tales. I dropped the pages from my hands. They had nothing to do with my father or my mother or my sister. They had nothing to do with me at all. There was nothing here. Nothing. All for naught, all craziness, all emptiness. I was in a grave, I felt, and I began to cry.

I tore the magazine up, threw my hands together as though in prayer, grabbed at my head and tore at my hair.

I shook convulsively. This, and my sobbing, didn't stop.

Not until it was dark anyway. It seems you can't mourn unless you know what you've lost, and that day, somehow, from finding nothing at all, I learned. I made my way back to Velden by flashlight.

FRANZ ROSEN

City
(from his diaries)

What a city we were. What an agglomeration. We were like a hothouse, that had grown under the Cold War's searchlights exotic flowers of every inappropriate variety. We were like a party that never stopped because when the dancing ended we knew we would die. We dined on wreckage. We were not afraid to beg. We continued our long tradition of believing either in nothing or too much.

HOLLY ANHOLT

Nils

ONCE I BEGAN TO MOURN, I mourned a lot. In my case anyway, mourning meant unlocking the loss from my mind, where it had sat like an urn on a mantel, always in plain view but never mentioned, almost from the time I was born. To me, mourning came to mean being here but also being there. It meant being without the Other, but also with the Other. Love was the engine of grief.

Unlocking love, unlocking grief. Unlocking grief, unlocking love.

I spent days in my room. I read various poets who'll go nameless. I packed. I watched TV. I spoke little to anyone. I forgot caring about who it was who betrayed my parents, or even if whoever it was was dead or alive. I caught a summer cold, and finally I rested.

And before I left, I called Nils. Funny the rules you make up for yourself when an affair is over, like I couldn't see Nils again but I could call him. I could always call him.

Or could I? I was so tongue-tied on the phone. I barely got my story out. He was a good sport about it all. This and that. He proposed some herbal thing for my cold that David swore by. And then: "I think it's a good thing…what happened to you."

"In the bunker."

"If it had happened before…I don't know…I guess it couldn't have happened before."

It was only then I remembered what I'd called him to say. I began to tremble again, the way I'd trembled in recent days, the way you might if you were carrying something you imagined of unusual value and became afraid, just for that reason, that you would drop it. I wished I could find, for just a moment, the unblinking grayness of his eyes, the color of the sea. "You know, if you don't mourn, if you can't mourn…I don't think you can know what it is that needs to be forgiven. Not fully, anyway. Not with a full heart… You may know who to forgive, or who not to, but you don't know the full loss…"

"Forgiven?" he said in the phone, and it sounded a little echo-y and hollowed out.

"It was what you needed from me, wasn't it?"

I felt I heard his shrug in the phone, I felt I saw the denial in his eyes.

"Then…then…Nils, I forgive you. For everything, for whatever…But mostly for everything you never did but think you're responsible for anyway… Your life is so hard. You're so hard on yourself."

Now he laughed. "Of course I'm not," he continued to laugh.

Then I kissed the receiver, and I believe I heard the sound, though I cannot tell you what such a sound would be, of his lips touching the plastic receiver at the other end of our connection.

Good-bye, Nils.

ABOUT THE AUTHOR

Jeffrey Lewis's four novels that make up the Meritocracy Quartet chart the progress of a generation from the '60s through the '90s. The first book of the quartet, *Meritocracy: A Love Story*, won both the Independent Publishers Book Award for General Fiction and the *ForeWord* Book of the Year Silver Award for Fiction. *Meritocracy* (1960s) is followed by *The Conference of The Birds* (1970s), *Theme Song for an Old Show* (1980s), and *Adam the King* (1990s). He won two Emmys and many other honours as a writer and producer of the television series *Hill Street Blues*. Jeffrey Lewis lives in Los Angeles and Castine, Maine.

Also by Jeffrey Lewis

Meritocracy: A Love Story

Summer 1966: a small group of recent Yale graduates gather in a Maine summer cottage. Harry Nolan, the son of a United States senator about to enter the US Army and Sascha, his beautiful young bride, represent the apex of their generation. Sascha has men falling for her 'up and down the eastern seaboard', and Harry's friends are convinced that he will one day be President. The narrator is Louie, whose unspoken love for Sascha is like a worm, cracking apart every innocent assumption. An aura of power, earned and unearned, assumed and desired, hangs over this Ivy League world and the events that ensue are fateful for the characters as they are emblematic of the era they grew up in.

The Conference of the Birds

In the late 1970s Manhattan, God is dead. A group of New Yorkers, as brash and defiant as their chaotic, bankrupt city, come together to explore the void left behind. Among them are the shy and sweet-natured Bobby, a gifted cartoonist and the group's mascot; Maisie, the acid-tongued rich girl who is fighting a two-front war against mental instability and Hodgkin's disease; the narrator Louie, a very nearly accidental pilgrim torn between his friends and the purpose that has engulfed him; and their austere leader Joe, a saint to some, a pervert to others. Is it self-discovery they seek, or oblivion?

Also by Jeffrey Lewis

Theme Song for an Old Show

Louie is a second-generation TV guy. Ascending rapidly, h
becomes a producer of one of the most beloved programme
in the history of television, the cop show *Northie*. But *Northi*
has fallen on hard times. Will it be cannibalised for one las
big tune-in, or will it be allowed to conclude its run in dignity
Jeffrey Lewis drives the story towards a conclusion that is a
astute and passionate indictment of our mass culture's coarsen
ing. Yet with the force of tragedy and the laughs of high farc
reduced to an absurdly tiny pixilated screen, this is also th
story of a man's last chance to find his father.

Adam the King

The wedding of billionaire Adam Bloch and Maisie Maclare
is the event of the year in Clement's Cove, Maine – a tow
in which the mansion-like 'cottages' of the summering elite si
side-by-side with the modest homes of working-class locals
When a misunderstanding between the couple and their nev
neighbors arises, a chain of events is set in motion that pits th
new rich against those just scraping by, outsider against old
timer, in an escalating struggle that can only end in catastrophe
Taut, swift, and startling, *Adam the King* depicts the inexorabil
ity of fate against the backdrop of the money-mad '90s.